Yolonde

and the Magic Silver Slippers

Michael Skyner

FUN

READS

Published in 2025 by FeedARead.com
Arts Council Funded.

A CIP catalogue record for this title is available from the British Library.

Illustrations by Canva

To the dyslexic kids

Glossary

Jambo hello

Okra sweet juice drink

Maasai nomadic people

Wali rice dish with coconut

Mandazi Kenyan doughnuts

Boma rural homestead

Ugali thick cornmeal stew.

Gari which means car

Swahili .main language of Kenya

Adumu. dance of the Maasai

Mwombokoa Kikuyu dance which is a dance performed by the elderly

Agikuyu dance which celebrates self-rule

Chakacha another popular dance

Joob JoobTree mythical tree whose fruit is believed to be magical

Savanna huge grasslands

Rift Valley The Rift Valley is part of an intra-continental ridge system that runs through Kenya from north to south of the country.

Somaliland country bordering Kenya

Khanga traditional Kenyan dress

Watusi dance craze popular in the 1960s

Hakuna Matata Swahili for no worries

Chapter 1

Katrina

This is me sitting on the number 27 bus going to Tottenham Hale, which is in London, by the way, near the High Street. It's Saturday, and on Saturday I normally play in the all-girls local football team, though we're open to boys joining, but so far none have been brave enough. "Not good enough for us girls see," the coach says.

But not today; today is the first Saturday of the month. I don't play football, so I always go to see my grandma instead. Grandma Wei, Wei, is cool and funny, not stuffy and old-fashioned as some grandmas can be. She is originally from Kenya, where all our family comes from, though I've never been myself. Maybe one day I'll go. Who knows? Kenya sounds like an amazing place, but like everywhere, it has its problems.

Ding ding. I love the sound the bell makes. This is my stop. Grandma Wei, Wei, lives just behind the High Street, close to Woolworths, or what was Woolworths before it closed down. Grandma Wei, Wei, would sometimes take me there and treat me to pick-and-mix sweets when I was little. She now lives in sheltered housing. It is for retired people. Want to come? You won't regret meeting Grandma Wei, Wei. Here we are number three. I'll see if she is at home.

Sometimes she goes shopping, but she always leaves a note on the door. 'Gone shopping back in one hour.' I tell her she shouldn't do that, as it tells bad people that there is no one at home. One should not encourage burglars. Grandma Wei, Wei, says I'm just a fusspot and not to worry. She even leaves a spare key under the doormat. The first-place bad people will look. I tell Grandma that she might as well leave a note saying, 'Dear bad people, please come and take all my things; there is a spare key under the mat just for your convenience.'

Do you know what Grandma Wei, Wei, says to that? I worry too much. OK, whatever, but this is Tottenham you know. To which Grandma Wei, Wei, responds. "Yes, but compared to Nairobi – the capital of Kenya, Tottenham is as safe as the inside of God's church." I'm sure that God always manages to lock his door. Anyway, today she's in.

"Hello Grandma."

"Jambo Katrina, it is good to see you again, child. Come in, come in; I have a treat for you today."

Jambo is Swahili for hello or how are you? We go into the front room, which Grandma calls the parlour. But it is the smells that are coming from the kitchen that really get me excited. I can tell from the aroma that Grandma is making Wali, which is a rice dish with coconut, and it is one of my favourites. But there is something else.

"Grandma, is that mandazi I can smell?" Mandazi are Kenyan doughnuts that are gooey and sticky. They're delicious and absolutely my all-time favourites. "You know I don't like doughnuts, don't you, Grandma?" Grandma Wei, Wei, starts to laugh. A belly laugh so deep it makes her whole body shake and wobble. Like a giant jelly. I laugh too; it's impossible not to, it's so catchy.

Finally, the tears of laughter stop, and Grandma Wei, Wei, speaks. "If I don't get into that kitchen, child, we won't be having anything for lunch except cold ham." Still chuckling, Grandma Wei, Wei, bustles into the kitchen while I lay the table. Later, we sit on the sofa like a couple of stuffed birds because we are so full. Then Grandma brings out the doughnuts, and it isn't long before I'm groaning. Four is too much, but I defy you or anyone to resist Grandma Wei, Wei's, doughnuts. We snooze, and then in the afternoon, we play a game. It's the same game every time.

I've always been fascinated by all the knick-knacks, bits, and bobs that Grandma Wei, Wei, has in her front room. They are all things that remind her of her childhood in Kenya and are her most precious things. The front room is full of them. Grandma Wei, Wei, allows me to choose one and then tells me a story or tale about it.

I don't know if the stories are true or not, but once Grandma Wei, Wei, begins her story, you do not want her to stop. Last time I was here, I chose a Maasai doll dressed in traditional dress and beads. The colours are amazing. The brightest blues, greens, and reds you've ever seen. Grandma told me how the Maasai, who are nomads – that is, people who have no permanent home – would travel hundreds of miles in search of new places to rear their cattle. And they are extremely tall; many are well over six feet, including the women. I am fascinated.

We've more or less talked about all the knick-knacks in the room, so I started to ask Grandma about the people in the album of photos she has on a small occasional table.

Grandma Wei, Wei, says they are her relatives.

"My family in Kenya; your family, Katrina."

Grandma fascinates me with tales of silly uncles, funny cousins, and her husband, Grandpa Wei, Wei, who sadly passed away ten years ago. But there was one picture that always intrigued me. It is a picture of a young girl in a dancing tutu and silver slippers. She appears to be receiving a big trophy at some big hall. I would often ask Grandma Wei, Wei, about the girl and who she was, but Grandma Wei, Wei, would shake her head and say it's not important and tell me to find something else. But not today.

"Grandma, you have told me about everything in the room but not who the girl in the picture is. Who is she, Grandma, and what is her story?"

Grandma Wei, Wei, sighed. She looked straight at me. There was a sad look in her eyes. She seemed to be thinking. Finally, she said "You really want to know?

"Yes, Grandma, of course," I said excitedly. I knew there was something special about the girl in the picture, but what it was, I couldn't say.

"Very well, child, I shall get you some more okra juice and tea for me, and then I shall tell you all about the girl in the picture.

I gulped down my juice and waited expectantly.

"Who is she, Grandma?"

"Her name is Yolonde, and she is the girl with the magic silver slippers."

"The what . . .?"

Chapter 2

Grandma begins to tell her tale

"Long ago there was a little girl who lived in a small village just outside Nairobi, which is a big city and the capital of Kenya, which is, as you know, on the east coast of Africa and is the place from which all of us Wei, Wei's, come from. Kenya is a large country, much larger than Britain.

"The village is called Matobi. It is a small village and extremely poor. Every day Yolonde would rise with the sun and walk one and a half miles to collect water from the local well, and then, with the pitcher of water on her head, return back home to help feed the chickens and get her two brothers and sister up, dressed, and ready for school while her mother made breakfast."

"One and a half miles, Grandma, she walks one and a half miles. Every day?"

"Yes child, but not one and a half. You are forgetting about the return journey with the pitcher full of water, which is very heavy to carry on your head, particularly if you are just a small child. So, it's three miles or five kilometres to you, and then she has all the other chores to do before she herself sets off to school."

"Three miles . . . Three miles . . ." I chewed the words over, trying to imagine what it would be like to carry water all that way and on your head. "I'll never complain about the tap water again, Grandma." Grandma Wei,

Wei, chuckled. Her whole upper body wobbled.

"Yes, we are indeed most fortunate to live in a country like Great Britain. We must count our blessings. But Yolonde never complained; it's what she was used to. Although she did pray every day that the village could have a well that was nearer, nobody would want to do what she and the other women of the village had to do.

I frowned. "What about the men, Grandma? What are they doing? Why do they not help?"

Grandma Wei, Wei, did something I had never seen her do before. She snorted, and tea flew out of her nose.

Chapter 3

Yolonde

Grandma Wei, Wei, continues to tell her tale in the traditional Kenyan story-telling tradition of using the first person, as if the subject of the story is telling it herself.

Hello, my name is Yolonde, and this collection of mud huts and thatched roofs is my village, Matobi, where I live with my sister Ukrem and my two brothers Akra and Pauli in our very own Ocha, or rural home. Akra and Pauli are quite little, so my sister and I help Mama out with the chores and looking after the chickens. I only mentioned the thatch roofs cos according to my Great-Aunt Matooba, everyone in the UK lives under a thatch roof too. I'm not sure if that is true, but it is what she says, so it must be.

Matobi is just outside Nairobi, the capital, and sometimes we can take the bus and visit the Big City, as we call it. But that is a rare treat, as we are always busy with the business of staying alive. If the rain comes, the crops are good, and the cattle are fed, then life is good, but if the rain fails, and it does fail often, then . . .

But let us not dwell on bad things. Life here is sweet. You see, it all depends on how you look at things. Mama says, "Yolonde, is your glass of okra juice half full or half empty?" She would say, "See, it is how you look at things," and Mama always makes sure we see things as being half full. Which is a good thing considering.

Then it's off to school, which is luckily on the bus route. Sometimes the bus does not come, and then we face a long walk. But you get used to it. I expect you have to walk a long way to school in the UK, or are there many buses? My Great-Aunt Matooba says that in the UK there is one bus for every person, and if my Great-Aunt Matooba says this, then it must be true. That is an awful lot of buses.

After school, while my two lazy brothers play and fight, my sister and I have to help Mama grind the millet for the evening meal. Today it is Ugali, which is a thick cornmeal stew. My favourite, though, is Wali, which is a rice dish with coconuts. We don't have Wali too often, as it is difficult to get hold of the coconuts unless you have money. And that is a big problem here in Matobi; we never seem to have enough of it, and that is because of one thing my Mama says – well, all the women of the village actually – and that one thing is men.

I haven't mentioned them up to now as it makes me quite angry. You see unlike the women who have to look after the children, tend to the animals and crops, prepare the food, mend clothes, and keep house, the men, well, the men just sit about. The old ones sit shading themselves under the big trees avoiding the afternoon sun. You can hear their laughter as they play dominoes, telling tales and stories from the Old Days. That's OK, they're old.

It's the younger ones who really make me mad, although we are not allowed to say anything. They sit around playing cards, drinking, swearing, and sometimes going off to the Big City to get up to no good, so Great-

Aunt Matooba says, and if she says it, then it must be true. Why do we allow this? Good question. The answer is in our culture, Mama says. In the past, the men would hunt and bring the meat while the women did the rest. Now they don't hunt, and we buy meat from the meat shop when we can afford it, which isn't often.

Some of the men work in the Big City and are good providers, but they are few. In the Big City, even where the men are good providers, the women still do most of the work, but out here in the sticks, most just sit about and create trouble for us. It's worse when they drink. And that brings me to my biggest nightmare—my stepfather.

Chapter 4

Drunken fool

The first I know he is back, is when I hear the front door being kicked open and a chair being thrown about the room. Then there are the cusses. When he uses bad words, I know he has been drinking, which is pretty much all the time. I hide in my bedroom, which I share with my brothers and sister, to keep out of the way. They are already there. At the first chance, my brothers leap out of the open window and leg it.

"Fetch me some food," he shouts. "I'm starving. Why am I waiting?"

"Your supper is with the dog," says Mama from the next room.

"What?" he roars.

Mama bustles in and challenges him. "If you were here on time then there would be food, but as you never tell me when you are coming home, then how can you expect food?"

It is the same argument they have every time. First, he asks for food and then they argue about money, cos he never has any.

Henri – for that is his name – cusses again and sweeps everything on the table onto the bare floor. "I said I want some food," he snarls. Mama shouts. I know what is coming.

"Yolonde."

"Yes, Mama."

"Heat up the stew up for this fool."

"Yes, Mama." I go unwillingly into the room and across to the kitchen. I know what's coming next. He grabs me by the arm.

"Ah, Yolondo, how is my little girl?" I turn my head away from his dragon breath and squeal as I fight to get loose from his grip.

"Leave the girl be!" shouts Mama, and he reluctantly lets go.

"My name is Yolonde," I shouted, as I squeezed past him into the kitchen and placed the stew on the fire.

"Whisky!" he shouts back. "Fetch me a whisky."

"There is no whisky, you drunken fool, you drank it all," says Mama, placing a glass of okra juice in front of him.

He eyes the okra as if he is looking at the devil. Then he sweeps the glass of okra juice onto the floor to join the rest of the things he has already swept there.

Mama gives him a look. I have never seen Mama look so angry before. Well, not since the last time he was here drunk.

Suddenly Henri stands up. He looks at us and around the room as if wondering why he is here. He has mad, wild staring eyes. You can see the whites.

"If you gave us more money then, we would have whisky for you to waste your money on. But as you always drink it away before you get here, then there is no money for whisky." Mama stares at him as if he is a ghost.

He raises his hand as if he is going to strike Mama but stops when I scream.

"Go to hell," he says, as he lurches out through the door.

"You are already there," says Mama. "Drunken fool."

When he is gone, I feel relieved. One blessing is that it will be weeks before we see him again.

"Why do you put up with him, Mama?"

Mama gives me the look. The look that says enough, Yolonde, we will speak no more of this.

It wasn't always like this, though. When Mama first met Henri, he was so handsome and would bring us treats and make us laugh. He was generous with his money, too, and so polite. Which is why Mama fell in love with him, well, liked him anyway. Nobody could ever replace the love Mama had for Papa. Of course, this was before we knew that Henri had a drinking problem.

Then he would change into a monster. At first, he would be so sorry for his behaviour, and Mama would forgive him. Then the nice Henri would return. But it didn't last; the monster would come back until it seemed the nice Henri didn't exist anymore.

"What would I do for money, child?" Mama would say in reply to my question: Then I would say: "But he never gives us any." And that would be that.

I switch the stove off. "What shall I do with the stew, Mama? Shall I save it for tomorrow?"

"No, give it to the dog when it has cooled."

"The dog?" I ask.

"That stew is days old, child, and it is not fit to eat."

"But why did you . . ." I paused when I realized I knew the answer. Mama and I both laugh while my sister just stares at the mad women.

Chapter 5

Dancing queen

I have loved dancing ever since I can remember. All I need is to hear music, and I'm off. Sometimes when Mama is outside, I will switch the old radio on to one of the more, let's say, trendy – I think you call it that in the UK – stations. Then I'm dancing like a banshee – that's a mad ghost, by the way.

I dream of being a professional dancer and performing in one of the shows in Nairobi, our capital. I can hear the applause as the crowd goes wild at my solo performance. Flowers are thrown onto the stage. Words are written about me in the papers. People ask for my autograph, which I graciously give of course. I, Yolonde, am the talk of the town. I am the envy of all my friends, who are mad with jealousy. There is just one problem with my fairy tale: I can't dance.

Oh, yes, I can jig up and down and thrash about. I can bop until I drop. But as Mama says, I will never be a dancer because I have two left feet. I think it means my feet won't work together. But I don't care. "One day, Mama, you'll see. All the world will know how great a dancer I am.

Mama is used to this by now. She is not one to discourage me but does so, I think, as an act of kindness. Mama says it is time to kop, which means to study, as she is convinced there is only one way to better oneself, and that is through learning.

"The dancing will have to wait until the elephants' ball, Yolonde." Well, we all laughed at that one.

See what I mean? She doesn't exactly discourage me, but I think she is afraid I will get hurt.

"What about lessons, Mama? I could always take lessons." I show her an old cutting from the local paper. There is an advertisement for dancing lessons for twelve Kenyan dollars a month. Mama has seen this cutting many times, which is why it is so worn, and the answer is always the same.

"I would love to child, but we cannot afford it."

What Mama doesn't want to say is that even if she could, I am a hopeless dancer. But I am ditermened. This is a long word I learned recently at school; it means never give up. Yes, I know; I have learned how to say the word but not yet how to spell it. But as my Great-Aunt Matooba says, if you can be understood, does it matter if you can't spell? And if my Great-Aunt Matooba says it, then it must be so, for she is incredibly wise.

"What if I saved up money from chores so I could have lessons, then I could go couldn't I?"

There is sadness in Mama's eyes, and she tries to hide it, but I see it. She sighs.

"You know I would if I could, Yolonde, but I simply cannot afford lessons."

"I know, Mama." I try not to show my disappointment. This is another long word I have learned, but for some reason, I can spell this one, although sometimes I leave out the second p. I memorized it by saying one sock and two parrots. Get it: one, s, and double p.

I have an idea. "What about Great-Aunt Matooba? She might have chores for me, and then she could pay me." I give Mama my biggest smile. It is my smile of hope. Mama looks at me for a moment, and I hold my breath.

"All right, child, I will ask, but I make no promises."

"Yes!" I shout inwardly to myself. Result. "Thanks Mama." Of course, it doesn't mean that Great-Aunt Matooba will be able to help, but it is a start. As Great-Aunt Matooba says: "Where there is a will, there is always a way." And I'm so willing, I think my chest will burst out soon with the pain.

Chapter 6.

Nice friends and nasty girls

Sometimes on Saturdays, when time and Mama's pocket allows, which isn't often, she lets me go to the big shopping mall in Nairobi with my friends from school, Twani and Joshi.

I sit under a banana tree, eating a delicious banana, while I wait at the bus stop. In Kenya, banana trees grow everywhere, so I suppose you can never really go hungry, so long as you like bananas. You can never have enough bananas, but too much of a good thing can make you sick. And sick of bananas too.

I plot and scheme, thinking up ways I can earn money for my dancing lessons. Perhaps I can rob the bank. I see myself in a large hoody holding a pretend gun and saying, "Stick 'em up." I shake my head as I am led away to jail. No, that idea won't work. There has to be another way.

The growl from the yellow bus distracts my thoughts as it pulls up at my stop. I get on quickly before the fumes from the old rattler choke me to death. Twani and Joshi are already there as they live further out.

"Jambo, Yolonde," they call out. "Jambo, Twani, Jambo, Joshi," I reply, which means, as you know by now, hello. I sit down excitedly. There is nothing more exciting than going on an adventure, and an adventure into the Big City with my best friends is about as exciting as it gets. We talk about what we are going to do when we get there. Twani says she hopes to buy a green tank top she has seen, as it is on sale. While Joshi is after some trainers.

"Where did you get the money for the trainers?" I ask. I know that Twani helps out sometimes in her uncle's shop and saves every penny she gets, but Joshi? He definitely must have robbed a bank, I think.

"I saved all the money I got for my birthday," he replies, "plus, I have been helping Papa in the fields."

And He pays you? thinks I. I think of all the chores I have to do around the house. I know Mama gives me some pocket money when she can, but that is rare these days. I look at Joshi, slightly ashamed of my creeping envy, which I try not to show in my face. If he has noticed, he pretends not to.

He must have had a strong will to wait all this time. All that money would burn a hole in my pocket, that is, if I had a pocket, which I don't. I just have a small purse that I carry around on a strap, so I don't lose it – another one of Mama's bright ideas to make sure I don't lose things.

It is so easy to lose things in Nairobi, and then, of course, there are always people – bad people, Mama says – who will help you lose your purse if you are not too careful. As if I don't know that Mama means thieves, but for some reason, Mama does not like to say the word thief.

"And what about you, Yolonde?" asks Twani as we get off the bus, thankful that we haven't choked to death from the fumes. "What are you hoping to buy?"

"Oh, nothing much," I reply, "just looking."

"Not looking for anything specific, like dancing lessons?" Joshi asks teasingly. He knows me so well. There is a dance studio in the mall, and every time we go past, I always enquire about lessons and always the same thing happens; they are too expensive. Even if I saved up my pocket money for ten years, it would not be enough. Not that I have any. Still, it doesn't hurt to dream, so my Great-Aunt Matooba says, but in my heart, it is hurting. It hurts really bad.

We pulled up outside the dance studio. There is a notice on the door. It is about a dance competition open to all. One-dollar entry fee. Now that I can afford, I think.

"You should enter," says Twani.

"Yes, you should definitely enter," says Joshi.

"Yes, I will absolutely enter," I reply. I can see myself standing on stage receiving the winning trophy or whatever you receive when you win a dance competition, and then my heart sinks as I hear familiar voices.

"Well, if it isn't skanky Yolonde."

"The girl who thinks she can dance."

"Not with those two left feet, she can't."

I turn to see Sumba, Yokta, and Peetree. Three girls from school who are definitely not my friends. They are the cool gang or so they think. I once tried to befriend them in the hope of joining their little gang. Some hope.

They don't allow skank girls into their little world, they said, and that was me, humil . . . humil . . . humiliated, phew got there in the end. Now they always give me the putdown whenever they see me. I ignore it, of course, but it is not so easy to let their barbed comments get to you. Especially when it comes to my dancing. I am sensitive that way.

They look me up and down as if I am something nasty that has stuck to their shoe.

"I should take lessons if I were you," says Sumba.

"Lots and lots of lessons," says Peetree, grinning evilly.

"In fact, I should buy myself some new feet if I were you," says Yokta, laughing, but not in a nice way. The girls giggle as they push their way through us. And they call me a skank girl.

And all this because they saw me bopping in the school hall one lunchtime. They are suffering from the green-eyed monster, I think. Not realizing that anyone who has actually seen me dancing might agree that they have a point. I watch as they go into the dance studio. A picture of something with horns and goes moo comes to mind.

"Ignore them," says Joshi.

"They are stupid girls," says Twani.

"Yes, really stupid." I agree, but perhaps they are right. Perhaps I should take lessons, but how can I afford them?

Chapter 7

Great Aunt Matooba

Two weeks later, I find myself finally turning into Agave Drive. It has taken me a long time to walk there. There being no direct bus, and besides, I have already had my bus treat for the month.

I open the gate and enter the garden of my Great-Aunt Matooba. Great-Aunt Matooba is rich. How do I know this?

Firstly, she is rich because she has a gate.

Secondly, she is rich because she has a garden.

Thirdly, she is rich because she has a veranda and a real tin roof on her bungalow, not straw like ours.

And finally, she is rich because she has a rich husband who owns a motor spares shop in Nairobi. They also have a Gari, which means car, and that means rich indeed – see another English, English word. Although Great-Aunt Matooba says in the UK every household has two cars, and if Great-Aunt Matooba says it, then it must be so.

We all have to learn English, English, at school, as well as Swahili, because the UK once ruled Kenya and there are still many English people who live up in the Highlands. That is the hilly central part of Kenya, where it is nice and pleasant and not too hot, which is how they prefer it. Although I would not like it at all – far too cold.

But that is not why we have to learn English, English. That is how they speak English in the UK. I'm sure you are confused, and I would not blame you for being so. English is the second language in Kenya, and English is spoken all over the world, almost, but you knew that, didn't you? Here, we speak a kind of local or pidgin English, but not like an actual pigeon, obviously.

I hug the mandazi - doughnuts - close to my chest and put the other gifts and cloth on the floor. Mama hopes Great-Aunt Matooba will use the cloth to make into dresses which Mama will then be able to sell at the market. I swear the cloth has made a dent on my head; it is so heavy. Then I knock on the door

"Come in," says a voice. "It's open." I pull open the outer fly trap door and push open the inner door, which is made of wood and very heavy. Inside, it is dark and cool. I can hear fans blowing, and light is streaming in through the window blinds. Compared to the scorching heat and blinding sun outside, the inside is like being in a cool box.

"I'm in the kitchen, child," says the booming voice of my aunt.

I go in and find my aunt bustling in front of the stove, from which the smell of something delicious is wafting up. My aunt turns and dusts her hands in her apron. "I am preparing Karanka stew with chapati for lunch, Yolonde; I hope you like it." I put my heavy burden on the chair as directed by my aunt.

Like it, I love it; another one of my favourites. "Oh, yes, Aunt, I love it." My face is beaming. Beaming because it is good to spend time with Great-Aunt Matooba, who is wise and who is also going to be the solution to the problem of the dancing lessons, although she does not know this yet.

"I'm sorry Naga was not at the door to greet you; it is her day off. So, you have got me to prepare the food and take care of you."

Naga, Naga, who is this Naga, and why is she having a day off? Oh, no, the penny drops. Naga must be a servant, and if my Great-Aunt Matooba has a servant, then my plan is well and truly sunk.

"You have a servant, Aunty?"

"We don't say servant, Yolonde; we prefer to say helpers these days, and yes, I have a helper. All the well-off households have them in Nairobi." I stare at my aunt until it seems rude. See, I told you she was rich.

"Are you all right, Yolonde? You seem far away. Come, bring your things; we will go and sit out on the veranda, and you can show me what you have brought." I stop gawping and follow my aunt out onto the veranda. My aunt carries a tray with a jug of sweet lemonade and some small cakes. She tells me to sit in the swing chair and hands me a drink. "Help yourself to some cakes." I grab a couple and then notice, or rather feel, the coolness of the glass. Something is rattling in my drink. O.M.G., real ice. See, I told you – rich.

After a delicious lunch, Aunty turns to face me.

"Now, Yolonde," says my aunt, turning all serious, "tell me why you are here."

Chapter 8

Aunty to the rescue

"I need dancing lessons, Aunty." I try to look Great-Aunt Matooba in the eye to see her response, but my eyes are diso . . . disobedient which means they won't do what I ask and are staring at the floor. I look up when Aunty speaks. "I know, child."

"You know?" I stare at my aunt, my mind racing with crazy thoughts. Is Great-Aunt Matooba, as we say in Kenya, a wise woman? These are women who, among other things, have the gift of seeing into the future. I think in the UK; you call them witches. Great-Aunt Matooba says the UK is full of witches and wise women who fly around on broomsticks and have a black cat. And if my Great-Aunt Matooba says it, then it must be so.

"Of course, I know, child; your mother says you talk of little else. We all know you are mad about your dancing." Aunt Matooba's face cracks open into an enormous smile. I wonder what my aunt is thinking. I do not have long to wait for the answer. "And how can I help you with the lessons?" There is a big twinkle in her eye.

I splutter. "Well, er, I was wondering if you had any chores I could do so that I could earn enough to pay for the lessons, but I did not know that you had a servant, I mean helper." I quickly correct myself.

My aunt stares at me for a long time. I can almost see the wheels turning in her huge head. But if I can see the wheels, I can't see what they mean. Finally, with a big sigh, like all the air going out of a balloon, my aunt speaks.

"That is most kind of you to offer Yolonde, but . . ."

There is always a but.

"Even if I did not have Naga, I cannot see how you would be able to do any chores. You have your own chores to do at home do you not? And it is a long way for you to come. Then there is school, or did you forget about that?"

No, obviously, I think to myself and then … how could I be so stupid? If my face becomes any longer it will surely fall onto the floor. I look up at my aunt feeling foolish. "Sorry, Aunty, I didn't think, I guess." I notice my aunt is still smiling.

"How much are these lessons?" she asks.

"What, er, twelve dollars, a month Aunty."

"And the competition, how much to enter?"

"A dollar," I reply all confused.

"Tell you what, Yolonde, I have some mail that I need to take to the post office." I would be most grateful if you would do that for me, and then we can have some tea upon your return."

"No problem Aunty." Well, you have to show willing, do you not? My aunt shuffles off to fetch the mail. She returns shortly with an enormous bag. When my aunt said mail, I thought she meant a letter or two. Not this great big bag of letters and parcels which I'm struggling to keep on my shoulder. Does my aunt know everyone in Kenya? Is that why she has so much mail? I walk down the drive and then struggle back up again. Aunty is still sitting on the veranda. "Er, where is the post office?" I ask.

Three hours later, I returned, dusty, sore, and aching all over. Even the bits I didn't think I had are aching. There are delicious smells coming from the kitchen, and I'm drooling. I give Aunty the receipts and change. She asks if I have any problems. I decide not to tell her that every few hundred yards I would stagger to a stop and have to rest, and this from a girl who can walk up to three miles with a pitcher on her head.

My arms ache in a way I didn't think was possible. I also didn't tell her that the postmaster had to do everything for me, as I got into a terrible muddle. But he was truly kind and patient, even though there was a big queue.

"Get a move on, girl."

"I haven't got all day."

"I'm growing old here."

"If you don't all pipe down, I will refuse to serve you; just be patient," says my new friend the postmaster. Well, that shuts them up. They are quieter than the Great Rift Valley, a big desert valley where nobody goes.

"You have done well, child," says my great aunt after we finish a delicious meal of rice and chicken. "Now I must pay you. Hold out your hand." I do so and look astonished as my aunt counts out thirteen silver dollars.

"What, no, Aunty, I can't." For one thing, my Mama will go nuts if she finds out.

"Consider it a loan, child; you can pay it back out of your winnings when you win the competition." My aunt has that big twinkle in her eyes again. Of course, my aunt has no intention of asking for the money back. But I don't know that. I also don't know that she has agreed to loan me the money with my

Mama's approval, and Mama will be making some dresses for Aunty as a way of repayment. But I will find that out later.

I continue to gawp at my aunt.

"Well, don't just sit there, child; haven't you got a competition to enter?"

"Thanks Aunty." I give Great-Aunt Matooba a big kiss on the cheek and run out of the house as fast as my eleven-year-old legs can carry me. Suddenly all the aches and pains vanish, as if they had never existed and though it is getting late, I know the dance studio will still be open, as they give lessons in the late afternoon and early evening. People out in the late afternoon may have noticed a swirling cloud of dust and legs. If so, that was me. When I arrive at the studio it takes me nearly two minutes to recover my breath.

Uncle Klobe gives me a brief tour of the studio, which is basically just a large room with giant mirrors at one end. There is a changing room attached and posters of famous dances from around the world. There are also pictures of traditional Kenyan dances and a picture of the president of Kenya, of course.

There is the Adumu dance of the Maasai, Kenya's famous giant nomads famous for their cattle and their colourful dress; the Mwomboko, a Kikuyu dance performed by the elderly; the Agikuyu, which celebrates self-rule; and other dances from the different ethnic groups of Kenya.

There are also posters of ballet and clogging, whatever that means, and more modern dances such as hip-hop and street dance. My head is giddy and spinning with the excitement of it all.

I am so giddy, in fact, that I do not notice the three nasty girls at the back of the studio eyeing me up and giggling. I ignore the "Two left feet have arrived," comment. I do not want to sink to such a low level as they inhabit.

I pay Uncle Klobe twelve dollars and ask when I can enter the competition.

"Whoa now, little Miss Keeny, first we need to see what you can do so I know what group to place you in. You can get changed through there." He points to a door. He notices my hesitation and looks down at my feet. "You have bought a dance outfit and shoes, yes?"

"Not exactly; I'm wearing my outfit, and these are my dancing shoes," says I, pointing down with my nose to my street slippers. The giggling at the back grows louder; it is in danger of breaking out into a full-on guffaw, which means a big laugh, any minute now.

"I see. OK, Yolonde, let's see what you've got. Start with the Adumu and the Chakacha, and then show me some street dance, and we'll take it from there.

"More giggling, and I'm sure I heard a "This should be good."

Uncle Klobe goes over to a machine in the corner and presses some buttons. After a few seconds, some music comes blaring out through hidden speakers. I recognize the music of the Adumu, the traditional dance of the Maasai. I have performed this dance many times in the school playground. I move my head in tune to the rhythm and then my legs as I jig up and down.

"Ah ha!" giggle the nasty ones from the back of the room. I am so absorbed by my dancing that I do not notice the reaction of the instructor. Uncle Klobe bends down and picks his jaw up from the floor. He presses a button and stops the music.

I hear the nasty ones say "Perhaps she should do the Mwomboko, the dance of the elderly; that should be slow enough for her. Hahaha."

"Enough," says Uncle. "Perhaps you should try some street dancing. You do know street dance, don't you, Yolonde?" More giggling, followed by "Wait for it."

"Of course," says I, wondering what on earth is street dance. I don't have long to find out. Loud, throbbing muzak blasts through the speakers with a thumping, harsh beat. I get into my groove, my little legs going one way, my arms the other, and my head bobbing furiously up and down, totally out of sync with the music.

"Stop, stop, stop!" The muzak is switched off. Wow, it hasn't taken me long to impress the instructor.

There is sweat on the brow of Uncle Klobe. "OK, Yolonde, thank you. I think I know where I shall put you – in with the beginners. We need to start from scratch, I think.

"The nasty ones have collapsed laughing. Uncle orders them out.

Beginners, beginners, how can I possibly be put in with the beginners? I open my mouth to protest, but he stops me with his hand.

"Please come next week and remember to bring your costume and dancing slippers." I turn to protest but change my mind when I see the look on Uncle Klobe's face.

"Yes, coach," says I, "see you next week."

I walk down the steps, where the nasty ones are still pointing and laughing. I ignore them. How could I have been so stupid? In my desire to have lessons, I have forgotten something important. Where on earth am I going to get a dance costume and dancing slippers? I ran and caught the bus home. Aunty kindly provided the bus fare. "You have walked enough today, child." I sit down on the seat and avoid other eyes so that they don't see the tears. Now what do I do?

Chapter 9

Spill the beans

"Well, how did it go?" asks Joshi, as we walk home from school. I don't know if real sheep can look sheepish or what a real sheep looking sheepish will look like, but I'm definitely, absolutely, looking sheepish. See, more long words from the English lessons. And I think they are spelled right. If not, please look up the correct spelling for me and let me know.

"Come on, Yolonde, spill it," says Twani, using what she thinks is trendy street talk. I turn my head slightly away, sure that a fib is coming.

"Oh, the coach thought I was really good; he entered me straight away into the competition; no probs there," I reply with my own version of street slang.

Alas for me, both of them have seen my 'dancing'.

"Really!" says Twani, and we all laugh.

"OK, OK, I was terrible," I confess, "the coach put me in the beginners, but I am in the competition, so there." I feel better now that the truth is out. Great-Aunt Matooba says that it is always better to tell the truth than to lie, except, of course, when telling the truth hurts someone's feelings, then sometimes it is OK to lie, but better to tell the truth. I sense some confusion in Great-Aunt Matooba's words.

And my aunty senses my senses, if you know what I mean, so she adds: "In the UK, everybody always tells the truth." And if my Great-Aunt Matooba says it, then it must be true. But for once, I'm not so sure she is telling the truth. Is it me, or is this becoming confusing? What about fibbing – a little lie – is fibbing OK?

"Coming to the Mall tomorrow?" asks Twani. I have forgotten that it is the last Saturday of the month.

This has put me in a bit of a spot, as I've got my first lesson on Thursday and cannot afford the fare to go twice. So, I say, "Nah, sorry, Mama needs me to help outside the house." They both look at me suspiciously – another big word. I turned away, embarrassed.

So much for telling the truth. Little did I know how much not telling the truth was going to hurt big time in a way I never thought possible.

Chapter 10

Joob Joob tree

Today it is ridiculously hot. I know that you think it is always hot in Kenya. Sure, some parts are hotter than others. I've already mentioned the Highlands, where it can be most chilly, and the Savanna, which is extremely hot, but just lately it seems to be getting hotter every day. Great-Aunt Matooba says it is due to something called global warming, and if Great-Aunt Matooba says it, then it must be so.

The walk to the watering hole seems even longer today due to the heat. The sun is so strong; it pounds, pounds, pounds, down onto my head. I put my water jug down; it is so heavy. I spy a tree. It is very shady, and for the first time, I decided I needed a rest. First, I must check out the tree for snakes and . . . *other things*. In Kenya, we have the most dangerous snakes, and as for the *other things,* the less said, the better.

OK, so the tree is clear, I think, of creepy crawlies, snakes, and other nasties. And anyway, I don't care, as I am tired and thirsty – very thirsty. You know what it's like to be really thirsty, right? Your mouth goes so dry, it feels like a sand desert in there. Cotton mouth, my Great-Aunt Matooba calls it, and if she says so, it must be true, and, as I have had cottonmouth many times, I can say that it is so.

Cottonmouth is like having razor blades inside your mouth, and the only cure is water. Well, that is not a problem; I am carrying a water jug. I hear you cry. The thing is, I'm on the way to the watering hole and not returning, so no water. But . . . but . . .

This tree that I'm sitting under, and which is giving me such lovely shade is famous throughout Kenya. It is called the Joob, Joob, tree and has lots of large, dangly fruit hanging down from its branches. The fruit has a delicious-tasting liquid. It is very tempting.

But . . . but . . . that is not why the tree is famous. It is famous for something else. If you drink the juice, it makes you dream. But not just any old dream; it causes haluc. . . Ok, I think I'll wait until Advanced English, English, then I will be able to spell it properly.

Did I mention that Things of Magic is a Kenyan specialty? Folk Tales and superst . . . superst . . . anyway, you can look that one up, which is popular here. But I don't believe in super . . . super . . . whatsits, and I don't care as I'm desperate. So, I pluck a really juicy looking one and sink my teeth into its delicious flesh. Am I nervous, you bet? O.M.G., the relief as the syrupy liquid hits the back of my parched throat. Ahh! Now that's better.

Well, I've quenched my thirst – is that the right word, quenched? I'm going to close my eyes for a bit, but not too long, as Mama is waiting for the water. Anyway, you can never rest in Kenya for too long; the flies see to that. Flies are to us what rain is to the UK. Great-Aunt Matooba says it always rains in the UK, while in Kenya there are always flies.

Except in the Highlands, of course, there are not so many up there, so it is said. I would like to say more, but my eyelids are simply too droopy. Yawn! I'll speak to you later.

Zzzzzzzzzzzzzz

Well, that's better. I'm still sitting under the tree and looking around. The flies are still buzzing, but you get used to it. Apart from that, all you can hear is silence. I know what you're thinking. How can you hear silence, you ask? Silence cannot make a sound, can it? Otherwise, it wouldn't be silent, but there you would be wrong. It's difficult to explain, but the next time you are in a park or the countryside – what we call the bush – go deep away from the noise of people and cars, find a quiet spot, and listen.

If you listen carefully what you will hear is silence. Yes, maybe the odd bird twittering and the rustle of leaves in the wind, but mainly silence, and then you will understand. How have I become so wise; you are thinking? I know. It's what Great-Aunt Matooba has told me, and if she says so, it must be true.

There is something vast in front of my eyes. I'm looking at the great savanna of grasslands in Kenya, with the Rift Valley in the distance. There are herds of cattle and African buffalo, flocks of starlings, and the odd scavenger bird or vulture. I don't think you have vultures in the UK, but you do have starlings. Maybe they are the same starlings, as starlings migrate from the UK to Kenya for the winter. As for vultures, here they are extremely large. Mama calls them Nature's Waste Disposal Unit.

The Savanna is dotted with trees and the odd watering hole, which is vital to all living things but is drying up due to clementine change. I'm not sure I've got that right, but I think you know what I mean.

Chapter 11

Lion

Something catches my eye. Well, first it's the smell, then the something, and the something is a lion. A big, huge beast of a beast with a giant mane and a head so big it's hard to tell where its body is. Then it moves. OK, the body is equally big.

The beast is staring at me, and strangely, it seems to have a puzzled look on its face. Oh, and the worse bit is that the lion is only about twelve feet – roughly four metres – from where I am sitting. See, I know about metric and imperial measures. Clever or what? Not really, it's just that we use both here in Kenya.

Am I dreaming? Well, it certainly looks and smells like a real lion. I'm frozen with fear, and so is my breath, which I have been holding in ever since I first saw it. I gulp some air, then freeze again. Don't move. Don't move. Don't antag . . . antag . . . oh, to poo with Advanced English, English. I didn't mean to swear, but after all, it is a lion. Don't upset it. Yes, that will do.

"Hello, I haven't seen you here before."

"What?"

I swivel my eyes this way and that to see who is speaking. There is no one there, just me and the lion.

"Hey, I'm over here."

I look back at the lion. "Uh! Um . . . Did you just speak?" I cannot believe I am asking this.

"Yes, I believe I did," says the lion.

"But lions can't talk." Have I really just said this?

"This one can and I can tap dance too." The lion stands up on two legs, performs a little tap dance, twirls, and gives a bow. "Ta dah! How's that?"

I pinch myself and shake my head. My eyes are wide and staring. This cannot be happening. I wish Great-Aunt Matooba and Mama were here. My voice is hoarse and croaky as I try to speak. "But . . . a lion can't tap dance." I whisper like a ghost.

"I think we've just covered that."

I look down at the half-eaten fruit in my lap. It's the fruit; it must be, it's just a dream. But . . . just in case . . . I look nervously at the lion. "Are you going to eat me?"

"As tempting as that might be . . . no."

"Then what are you going to do to me?"

"I hear you want to learn how to dance."

"How do you know that?" I ask.

"Oh, we lions know a thing or two," says the lion, scratching. "Come on, we'll start with the basics and work our way up from there."

"But . . . but . . ."

My heart is pounding, and my eyes are full of terror as the lion on two legs takes me gently by the hand and leads me to a little clearing. A voice comes into my head, but it is not the lion's. "Relax Yolonde, the lion will not harm you, he is here to help you, do not be afraid." For some reason, the voice comforts me, and I relax . . . but only a little.

"Now, says the lion. I'll lead, and you follow . . ."

Chapter 12

Lion dancing

I cannot believe this is happening to me. I'm dancing, really dancing, and I don't seem to have two left feet anymore. Also, I can't stop and don't want to stop.

"We'll start with something simple," says the lion, "and take it from there."

The lion takes me through the basic steps for traditional Kenyan dance, followed by hip hop, jive, and the classical ballroom dances (cha cha, foxtrot, quickstep). Phew! I'm really breathless now. We kicked up quite a storm. But . . . but it can take years to learn these dances, yet here I am killing it like a pro. You don't believe me, do you? Here, I'll prove it. I'll draw you a picture of some of the steps, and then you'll have to believe me, huh? Finally, we stopped. I'm exhausted, but not the lion.

"Well, that's enough for today; call me if you want to learn more."

I watch as the lion trots off until he is out of sight. I sit down again by the tree and think about what has just happened. Did I dream it?

"Yolonde, what are doing there? You should be fetching the water. Your mother will be expecting you." I look up, trying to block out the sun. The face staring back down at me is a woman from our village.

"Sorry, Aunty," says I. We are not related – all the adults over a certain age are called either uncle or aunty out of respect.

"Walk with me this way child, I shall make sure you do your duty."

I walk alongside trying not to think of my encounter with the lion. I push it from my mind and think about something else. I wonder if children have chores to do in the UK. Great-Aunt Matooba says the UK is so rich the children do not have to do chores but still receive pocket money. This is an astonishing fact if true, but if Great-Aunt Matooba says it then it must be so. The children in the UK must be lucky indeed. Fat chance of it happening here, unless you are a male of course – I had to get that one in.

I talk to Village Aunty all the way back from the well. Until she says: "Enough child, I have never met anyone who talks so much," and leaves. I place the pitcher outside and go into my home. There's nobody in so I go to my room – the one I share with my sister and flop. I'm kaput.

Time to think . . . I think.

And then my sister comes and tells me the news . . .

Chapter 13

Very bad people

The school was closed for three weeks. That was to give us time to attend the funerals and say goodbye. To grieve is a word that Mama and Great-Aunt Matooba use. I did not understand what it meant until now.

"Thank goodness, you did not go to the Mall, Yolonde."

Mama is squeezing me so tightly that I think I'm going to suffocate. "Mama, I can't breathe." Mama relaxes her grip. But she has been doing this a lot since . . . It happened.

And now I, along with all the other kids, am banned from the mall.

"Let the child have some air, Sasi," says Great-Aunt Matooba. Sasi is my Mama's first name, but so rarely does she or anyone else use it that I forget for the moment who it is. It is Great-Aunt Matooba who addresses us children.

"Children, you must be brave and not cry. We must remember our loved ones with our heads held high."

Yeah, right, I've been crying for twenty-four hours, but I know that my aunt means well. We hear the noise of the buses approaching; it is time to go. Dressed in our best – well, our only – black clothes, we go outside. The whole family is gathered together, including the waste of space which is my stepdad. He at least has the decency to keep a little distance from us.

Outside, we join the entire village – well, all those who are old enough and able enough to go. There is only the sound of whispered voices as we climb aboard the buses that are to take us to the funerals. The sky is cloudy, which is rare these days.

As I look at the countryside while the bus heads towards the crematorium. (I had help spelling that one.) I think about what happened that day. Our village lost two children; others lost many more; and I lost my best friend Joshi.

"Bad people from Somaliland," so my Mama says. "Very bad people with guns and hatred in their eyes." Two hundred and sixty-nine people lost their lives that day. Many more were severely injured and would never be the same again.

Somalia is a large country next door to Kenya, but it has no proper government, and bad people or terrorists, as Great-Aunt Matooba calls them, have camps there, and they raid into Kenya, attacking tourists and now the mall. But Somalians are good people, so my Mama says. There are many Somalians living peacefully in Kenya; it is just the extrem . . . it is just the bad people.

At the funeral service, I held hands with Twani. Everyone is crying now, including me. Well, once one person starts, it makes us all cry. Twani had a lucky escape; she had gone into a shop to look at some clothes while Joshi waited outside eating a doughnut. When she heard the shots, she hid under a counter until the security people came and rescued her. It took hours, though, and Twani was terrified, as we would all be.

Especially when one of the gunmen walked into the store where she was. Twani held her breath so hard she thought she was going to die which if she had made a noise, she most certainly would have. But the gunman moved on waving his machete and gun in the air, shouting, and screaming, but at least Twani could breathe again.

A person came from Nairobi – a counsellor – I think Twani said, to help the children, who were there or who lost friends, cope. Twani said it did help a bit, but she still has nightmares about that day. I have some too. Sometimes it helps to talk and have someone listen.

After the service, we returned to the village. We all gather around for food and drink, paid for by Great-Aunt Matooba. But it isn't long before some of the children go off to play. Well, children have short memories, and things don't affect them the same way as adults. Mostly.

As for me, well, I am banned from going to the mall because it is closed anyway, and the dance academy is closed. So, when everyone has gone, I say my goodbyes to Twani and my drunken stepdad, who has been hitting the bottle ever since his return. I slipped away unnoticed, my thoughts turning once more to dancing and . . . to the lion.

Chapter 14

Oh dear

Life slowly returns to normal. Our school reopened, as does the shopping mall. But some things will never be the same. I can never go to the mall again without thinking about Joshi. So, I stopped going. But not to the dancing. After three weeks, the dance studio reopens, and I find myself standing once again outside sacred grounds. With one big difference . .

"Hurry up, Naga, I'm going to be late." I watch while Naga reluctantly shuffles her feet one in front of the other. "It's not my fault, Naga, remember." Naga has a face like the back of a baboon. This is the condition of my return to the dance studio. I am to be escorted, which means someone has to be with me, in case you didn't know. It was Great-Aunt Matooba's idea, and who is going to question Great-Aunt Matooba? But nobody thought of asking Naga, hence the dragging of the feet.

We go into the studio while Naga goes off to look around the shops. The skanky girls are there, but I don't care; I can't wait to show Uncle my new moves, as taught by Lion. "Hi Uncle," says I. He's not my real uncle, of course. If you remember, we call all men over a certain age uncle.

"Hello Yolonde, back for more punishment, I see."

"Pardon." Now pardon is a new word that I have learned in Advanced English, English. It means excuse me, or what did you say?

Great-Aunt Matooba says in the UK everyone says *pardon* and not *what,* which she says is common and vulgar. And if Great-Aunt Matooba says it, then it must be so. In fact, I find out later that the upper classes – what is known as the ar/is/toc/ra/cy in the UK - say what and consider pardon as vulgar. Did you see how I did that? I used silly bulls; aren't I clever? I guess it depends on who you are. Perhaps the upper classes are vulgar, but I wouldn't know.

There is a saying: Practise makes Perfect. And if only I had practised what the lion had taught me, then what was about to happen would never have happened.

"Now before class begins, does anyone wish to show me what they have been practising?"

My arm shoots up before my brain has a chance to know what is happening. Uncle's face drops.

"Yes, Yolonde," his voice betraying what he is thinking. "What are you going to show us?"

"Tango, Uncle," I reply.

"That is a complicated dance, Yolonde. Are you sure?"

"I know."

"But you need a partner, Yolonde."

"No need; I'll imagine one."

"But, but . . ." Uncle scratches his head. "Let me partner with you."

"I'll be fine, Uncle," I say, full of confidence, so keen am I to show my new moves. Uncle sighs and gives up.

"This should be good." I hear from the back of the class.

"Do you have your own music?"

"No Uncle, anything will do." Uncle goes over to the music player and selects a tango track. "Ok, when you are ready." The music starts, and I began to dance the tango that the lion showed me, and then, oh, dear. With the tango music still playing, I move on to hip-hop, where I dance with an imaginary partner. Uncle has given up. This is followed by the foxtrot, cha, cha, cha, paso doble, jive, and other dances I have learnt. But wait, something's not right. I'm foxtrotting where I should be tang going. I'm hip-hopping with ballet moves.

What the … My arms are doing the foxtrot, but my legs are doing the quickstep. Everything's mixed up. What is going on? Much later, someone from the class told me it was the funniest thing they had ever seen. Ever!

The class stared open-mouthed as I gyrated my tush, body, and legs flailing about in all directions. The music is switched off, and my humiliation is complete.

The silence is deafening. Then the skanky girls start laughing.

"Er, thank you, Yolonde, most er . . ."

I ran from the front of the class and out of the studio, tears streaming down my cheeks, my face red as a beetroot, the words "What a loser," from the skank girls screaming into my ears, and the sounds of laughter echoing. I run past Naga, who stares open-mouthed as I head out of the mall and into the street.

Chapter 15

Yolonde makes a discovery

With tears and snot on my face, my legs keep running down the road away from the mall and my recent humiliation. The stares from passers-by make me pause. I take out a much-used hanky and annihilate it. (Wow, how did I spell that one?) This is how . . . an/ni/hi/late, using silly bulls again. But at least my face is clean.

Slowly, my sobbing dies away, and my tears dry up – very slowly. Eventually, I find myself shuffling along one of the old rows of small shops that litter the outskirts of Nairobi.

I decided to walk and not take the bus. Besides this is my way home, and I often find myself staring at some of the shops when I'm on the bus. Now I have the chance to see them up close. These are local shops for local people, the type of shops people who can't afford to go to the mall go to, and for shopkeepers who cannot afford much in the way of rent.

I walk past run-down general stores, shoe repairs, greengrocers, and butchers, with the cheaper beasts hanging down from hooks outside. Yuck! There are also seamstresses – ladies who repair old clothes and places where women never go – betting shops where the foolish men lose all their money betting on stupid races, so Mama says.

There is also a cake shop, this is what I've had my eye on for some time, and I go inside to buy myself a treat. Problem . . . What can I get for fifty cents? Not a lot, it seems. I drool over cream swirly whirlies and chocolate ice buns, but the stale-looking doughy thing with a price tag of fifty cents does not appeal. "Er, do you have anything else for fifty cents?" I ask, not expecting much of a result.

The big, busty lady behind the counter stares down at me. "You're Yolonde, Sasi's daughter, aren't you?"

"Yes," I reply. I watch wide-eyed as she takes a spatula and picks up one of the chocolate-iced buns and places it in a paper bag. I'm still staring at it in my hand as she takes the fifty cents from me by way of payment. "But, but . . ."

"Sorry to hear about Joshi and the other children in the village. Give my regards to your mother."

I'm too stunned to say anything as, in a dream state, I stumbled from the shop, clutching my prize tightly in my small hand. I turned to look back at the shop, but the lady is serving another customer. I hope she doesn't think I was being rude. I skip a couple of steps but no further as I remove the prize from the bag and plunge one end of the bun into my mouth, smearing delicious cream onto my nose. Oh, my god, this is so nice. Uh! I bet it makes you wish you had one, doesn't it? Well, sorry, go get your own. This is all mine. Yum!

Finishing my treat, I skipped merrily down the street, all thoughts of Naga and my humiliation at the dance club are a distant memory. Suddenly, I freeze. Naga! Oh, my goodness, Naga will be going frantic searching for me, and then she will tell Great-Aunt Matooba, who will tell my mama, and then . . . I lick the last of the cream from my face. Oh, well, time to go home and face the music, I guess. Wait, something catches my eye. Not just any old something either.

I'm looking into the window of a run-down shoe shop. There are the usual tatty sandals and old men's shoes, many of which look second-hand, which they probably are. But it's what is sitting in the middle of the display on a cloth-covered shoebox that catches my eye. I'm looking at a pair of dancing shoes, or slippers, as the tag says. But not just any old slippers . . . They are silver with a silver buckle, which as I learn later, is what it is called, and it is how you fasten the shoes.

They are the most beautiful dancing shoes I have ever seen, much nicer than the ones the skank girls wear at the dance club, which, they claim, are really expensive. And certainly, a thousand times better than the rubbish ones I have. No, these are authentic, which means the real thing.

It's almost magical, the way the silver colour of the slippers sparkles and shimmers with the light. I'm breathless with excitement. Until I notice that, unlike the other sorry specimens on display, there is no price tag, one word stands out on the tag, and it's the word professional. Like a zombie in a daydream, I open the door of the shop and go inside.

Chapter 16

Magic slippers

Inside the shop, it is dark and dusty. All around, boxes are piled high, with pairs of shoes sitting on top. More piles of shoes are heaped together in bins. Other racks contain single shoes, so that no one will take them. I think you say pinch in the UK, or shoplift, as my Great-Aunt Matooba says. She says that the UK is a nation of shoplifters, and if my Great-Aunt Matooba says it, then it must be so.

But I think Aunty is confusing shoplifters with shopkeepers. 'A Nation of Shopkeepers' is the expression I read in one of my history books from the school library. It's the only history book in the school library, and its title is: The UK: A Nation of Shopkeepers. So, that's how I know. Actually, that is not quite correct; there is also a short book called The History of Kenyan Independence.

The shop bell must be an extremely quiet one, as I don't hear it ring when I enter, but somebody else does. From the back of the shop, a curtain is swished aside, and in waddles a large lady wrapped in traditional Kenyan dress called the khanga. I find myself trying not to stare. I failed badly.

She notices my look and frowns.

"Can I help you?" says the lady shopkeeper in a shrill voice; her eyes seem to go right through me.

It takes me a few seconds to recover my senses. "Er . ." "Yes?" she booms. I feel my legs beginning to shake.

"Er . . ."

"You've already said that."

In any situation when you find yourself panicking, my Mama says to take a deep breath. So, I do. "I . . . I . . ."

"Spit it out, child."

If this woman were to enter the Olympics out of impatience, she would win gold.

"It's about the dancing slippers in the window. I just wondered how much they cost." I finally managed to blurt it out.

To my amazement, the shopkeeper's face breaks into an enormous smile.

"Well, why didn't you say so, child?"

That's what I was trying to do.

The shopkeeper sweeps past and goes into the window. She returns with the slippers. She hands one over to me. I look at it in amazement. Up close, it is beautiful, and the silver shimmers in the dusky light – shimmer means shiny, in case you didn't know.

"They are handcrafted, you know," says the shopkeeper. I turn the slipper over in my hand, marvelling at the quality of the stitching.

I want them so badly, but my heart sinks in despair. I know I cannot afford them.

"How much?" pointless to ask.

"You ask how much they are when what you should really be asking is, will they fit?"

"But will you have my size? I'm only a size five."

"We only have the one size."

"Oh." My heart sinks beneath the waves of hope.

"Luckily for you, child, the size we have is a size five. Why don't you try them on?"

"Wha—?"

"Why don't you try them on?" The shopkeeper passes over the other slipper. I turn them over in my hands as if they were something magical.

"You can use that stool there." The shopkeeper points to a wonky old stool that looks as if it will collapse the moment you sit on it.

I sit down and put them on; they fit perfectly. It's as if they were made just for me. The slippers glow in the early evening light.

"Walk up and down, child."

I do as I'm told. The slippers are amazing. I feel like I'm walking on air.

"Well, what do you think?" asks the shopkeeper. As I don't respond right away, she frowns.

"They are amazing."

"Would you like to have them?" she says, smiling.

Is that a question?

"These are magical slippers, child; with these slippers, you will be able to perform any dance you wish. You can become the greatest dancer in all of Kenya, if not the world. If you believe in yourself, that is . . . do you believe in yourself?"

My open mouth says it all. I want these slippers more than anything. While I am staring at them, an image of the lion comes into my head. His head is nodding up and down as if he is agreeing.

"Yes," I say weakly, knowing in my heart of hearts I will never be able to afford them.

"Then they are yours, Yolonde," says the lady shopkeeper.

"Wha . . . but I can't afford them."

"To the child who believes in herself, the slippers are free. Besides, I have been trying to sell them for the past six months, and you are the first person to have shown any interest. To be honest, I was about to throw them away."

It never occurred to me to question why the shopkeeper should want to get rid of some exquisite slippers for nothing. Then again, I was too excited to question anything. The shopkeeper goes away and comes back with a box containing the magic slippers.

I rushed from the shop before she could change her mind. I shout, "Thank you, Aunty," as I leave.

I am so excited that I cannot stop laughing as I skip gaily down the street. Then I stopped abruptly. Feet first, body catching up a few seconds later.

Hang on, how did she know my name?

Chapter 17

Dancing queen

"Sorry Mama." I hung my head ashamed. But out of the corner of my eye, I secretly watch my Mama's reaction. I've just had the biggest telling off of course. Aunt Matooba was not at all impressed by my behaviour, and I owe a big apology to Naga, who had been going frantic with worry about my disappearance. It was Naga who told my mama.

"I should think so. What were you thinking? No, don't answer that; you clearly weren't thinking at all," says Mama. I receive my punishment of extra chores, and Mama says she is going out to see Aunt Matooba to apologize in person for my behaviour.

My eyes betray me. My mouth, more so. "Yes, I know I've done wrong, but let's keep it in proportion, shall we? It's not as if I've blown up the Mall, is it?" As soon as the words explode from my mouth, I wish I could take them back. But it's too late now; the cat is well and truly out of the bag. Mama glares at me.

"I'm really surprised at you, Yolonde," says Mama as she walks out, slamming the rotten old door behind her. It's barely hanging on its hinges.

I'm on my own, as my brothers and sister are at school. I should be at school too. But Mama is keeping me off to clean the house. She says I can go to school tomorrow. She knows how much I love school, and I'm dying to tell Twani about the slippers. The slippers

– I'd forgotten all about them, well, only for a few moments. I should have told Mama, but in the mood she is in, I do not think this is a good idea. Do you?

I rush to my bedroom and carefully slid the box out from underneath the bed. With excited hands, I open the lid, and there they are: the magic silver slippers. They seem to gleam and pulse or is it just my childish imagination.

Did I not see a twinkle of stars?

Of course, there's no such thing as magic, or is there? But to me, they are magical. Well, as I'm on my own, I might as well, you know, give them a go. I sit down and carefully place the slippers on my feet. Perfect fit. I stand and try to find balance. They are a fine pair of dancing slippers.

Hmm, what shall I try out first? I know the Watusi. I slowly twist and turn, and to my surprise, my feet respond exactly as they should. No gangly awkwardness; no two left feet; simply perfect rhythm and timing. I stop in shock, like a kitten when it first hears itself purr.

This is fun. I run through as many dances as I can remember, from street dance, hip-hop, jazz, tap, Latin, and modern. This is the 1980s, after all. I do a perfectly formed foxtrot with an imaginary partner. This is amazing. I twirl about while dancing a waltz. Followed by a paso doble. I imagine myself on the stage of a great theatre. The crowd is going wild for my performance. Then the announcer declares the winner. "Give it up for Yolonde." I blush and bow while being showered with flowers.

Something is wrong. Someone is watching me, but it's not the audience. "Yolonde." I hear my name being shouted very loudly. I pause in mid-twirl and open my eyes to see my Mama staring at me open-mouthed. Apparently, the bus didn't come; it had broken down again.

"Hi," I say weakly. I'm for it now.

"I thought I left you to do the cleaning." Mama pauses and points to my feet. "What are those?"

Oops, busted.

Chapter 18

Dance club

Well, I've scrubbed the kitchen sink, washed the floors, fed the chickens, and fetched the water, and I'm still grounded for two weeks. No biggie, as the dance competition isn't for another fortnight, so I've still got time. While I'm busy doing chores, I dance, I twirl, I pirouette, which means I leap, lunge, and . . . I think you get the idea.

My brothers and sister stare at me open-mouthed. They can't understand what's happening. How come I've suddenly gone from rubbish to super dancer in the blink of an eye? Well, I just say it's finally clicked and is the result of all the practising I've been doing. I can't tell them about the lion, can I? And although they can see I have a tatty-looking pair of dance slippers, they don't know they're magical, do they?

Mama doesn't seem to mind. She knows how important this is to me. But she has to show that she knows I have done wrong. Well, there's no gain without pain, as they say. But that's the point. There is no pain. With these magic slippers on my feet, everything is so easy. I'm going to nail this competition, and then it's the biggie. The Kenyan National Dance Competition, and then, who knows . . .

Uncle, my dance instructor at the dance club, has contacted Mama. He says it's important that I come to rehearsal as I have to dance with a partner. And as nobody wants to dance with me based on my previous performance, Uncle is going to partner me.

"No, I can't partner you in the competition, Yolonde; I'm the coach, but I will pair you up with the best." He pauses. "Well, with somebody anyway," says Uncle, scratching his head.

Charming!

I am finally released from my enforced imprisonment, and with Twani and a still unsmiling Naga in tow – can't blame her really – I arrive at the dance studios for the final run-through with Uncle.

Uncle takes no chances and puts me through my paces, starting with the easy steps and the simpler dances. I nail them. The lines on Uncle's forehead go from worry to surprise and then astonishment.

"You have been practising, Yolonde."

"I can do better than this, Uncle."

"OK," he says, and we go through the lot. The foxtrot, the cha, cha, cha, the paso doble, jive, quick step, rumba, traditional Kenyan dance, ballet, and jazz. Well, I do the ballet, not Uncle, as he's getting on a bit.

Uncle's face is now one of amazement, as I am dancing better than even him. I wish you could see the look on the skank girls' faces; their jaws have dropped so far, they are in danger of hitting the floor.

"Yolonde, this is simply amazing. I had no idea. You are now our lead dancer and shall be entering you for the pairs and the solo dances. I cannot partner you in the competition of course, but I will partner you with the best. Yolonde I think we have a good chance of winning this competition and if you keep this up . . ."

My face is in danger of being cut in two by my enormous grin.

A black cloud has risen from the back of the room. The look on the skank girls' faces has gone from malicious disbelief to sheer hatred. Never hate anyone. Hatred is a poison that comes back to poison the hater. But the skanky girls don't know that, of course.

Chapter 19

One week to go

It's a week to go, and we've been rehearsing like mad. There are the relay teams for the free dance and pairs for the formals, plus the individual slots, which are so important if we are to win. And, if we win, we are au-to-ma-ti-cal-ly - I think that is the right spelling - entered into the Kenya National Dance Competition, but I think I have already mentioned this.

Our confidence is high. Do you know this word? It means we are all convinced that we could win this competition; isn't that exciting? Winning is so important. Do you agree? Great-Aunt Matooba says it is not about winning but about taking part, which is important. And if my aunt says this, then I know it must be true. Let's face it. It was only a few weeks ago that I couldn't dance the hind legs off a donkey. I think that is the expression you use in the UK. Great-Aunt Matooba says there are many donkeys in the UK, but I'm not sure what she means by this.

I look down at my magic slippers; they are sending out little sparks of glitter and stars. This happens only when no one is looking. Clever slippers. I know we can win, and my heart is overflowing with happiness and joy. Is yours?

Great-Aunt Matooba says, "No matter what happens in your life, you should always try to be happy." She says life is like a roller coaster. There will always be difficulties. Good times. Bad times. Times of joy and times of loss. But it is important to strive to be upbeat. You have a choice. You can let important things upset you or remain upbeat; I choose upbeat. So should you.

I am puzzled by this; I can tell you. I mean, there will always be times when you are sad. You can't possibly be happy all the time, can you? I mean, I was sad when I lost Joshi at the mall when the bad men came. But Great-Aunt Matooba explains it to me like this:

"You must not let hatred and sadness upset you so that you cannot live a happy life. Hatred, envy, regret – these are all poisons. You must avoid the poisons." Now I think I understand what my aunt means, and if Great-Aunt Matooba says it, it must be so.

Chapter 20

Friday, one day to go

It's the day of the final rehearsal, and everyone is buzzing. Do you know this word, buzzing? See, we are not backward here in Kenya. We know all the trendy words, like posh, hip, and fab. This is the 1980s, after all.

I go to my locker to get changed. This is how important I am now; I have my own locker. But I must not be boastful; that means to brag. As Great-Aunt Matooba says, bragging and pride are also poisons, but a little bit is OK, I think.

"Hi, Yolonde."

"Hi, Twani."

Twani has come to watch me at a rehearsal. It is a great source of pride; I am most pleased. We chat about nothing; mostly boys as I open my locker. Yes, we do notice boys, you know – who is hot, who is not, who is in our dreams, who we might fancy. But I have no time for boys, for real. Not until the competition is over, and besides, Great-Aunt Matooba and Mama would kill me if I were seen with a boy. I am only eleven, after all. I take out my dancing costume and reach inside for my slippers.

"My slippers."

My magic dancing slippers are not there.

Chapter 21

Help

I searched everywhere I could think of, but of the slippers, there was no sign. What am I going to do now? Without the magic slippers, there's no way I'm going to be able to dance. I just know it. I can feel it in my bones.

Twani and Naga both help with the search. Uncle says he will find me a replacement pair, and they all say it is going to be OK. Except the skank girls, of course. They can barely contain the glee in their voices as they pretend to show concern.

The skank girls are having a field day at my expense. Do you know this expression? I read it the other day in a newspaper in the school library. I'm not quite sure what it means, but it seems to fit. If you know its true meaning, perhaps you will let me know.

Great-Aunt Matooba says all the houses in the UK have TVs. You must be rich indeed. We have TVs in Kenya, of course, but not very many, and certainly not in our village.

Hah! But what we do have are thousands of banana trees, as you know, all over Kenya. I bet you don't have banana trees growing in your backyard like we do. See, there are many advantages to living in Kenya, but having a TV is not one of them.

I'm sorry; I've just realized that my remarks about the banana trees might have come across as being boastful. And being boastful is one of Great-Aunt Matooba's deadly sins. So, I am sorry. I didn't mean to be boastful. Well, perhaps just a little bit. I know,

I know, pride is also one of the great deadly sins, according to my aunt. But is it wrong to take pride in one's country? I think not. Gosh, what a rebel am I?

Everyone is telling me it is going to be OK, but I know differently. Without my magic slippers, I will not be able to remember all of the steps. I will be like the donkey again, with the two left feet. I am in despair. Do you know this word? It means there is no hope. The competition is tomorrow, and in order to compete in the Kenyan National Dance Competition, we have to win all the categories: team, pairs, and individual. I am doomed.

Chapter 22

Saturday, day one of the competition

The competition is set over two days: the first day is for groups, and the evening is for pairs. Day two is for the individual categories, and I must perform my absolute best if we are to succeed in winning. No pressure, then, which is made worse, of course, by the loss of my precious – there's that word again – slippers.

Well, here I am waiting in the wings. My heart is in my mouth, not literally, of course; that would be impossible, not to mention quite horrific to look at. It is our turn next.

The first part of the competition is the group performance. We have chosen a modern jazz theme, performed to the music of popular jazz of the 1960s. You probably have not heard of it. It is called the Watusi.

Do you know jazz? It is a funny kind of music, as it seems very random when played. I certainly never heard of it before I joined the dance club. But if you are going to take dance seriously, then you must be familiar with all the different types of music that there are.

People think jazz is just for oldies, but it seems it is not so. There are many modern jazz dances performed by young people. Uncle says jazz music and dance are still extremely popular in the UK. I'm not so sure; this is the 1980s, after all. We younger ones would have preferred a more modern category. But Uncle is confident that ours is a winner. Let us hope so. I wonder if Uncle is too old for this. At least he will not be performing; as a former professional, he is not allowed.

Chapter 23

Feeling nervous

"Remember, you can do this; it doesn't matter what slippers you are wearing," I mumble.

Oh, but it does.

I am extremely nervous. Mama and Great-Aunt Matooba will be in the audience, along with Twani and most of my village. Wow! No pressure, then. Because there are a great number of entries, the competition is being held over two days. I think I forgot to tell you this. It means the pairs and individual performances will be held on Sunday, and the individual and overall winners will be announced Sunday evening. So, maybe there's still time to find my slippers. The replacement ones are pinching at the toes. This is not helpful.

It is our turn now. Wish me luck. I look down at my feet where the magic slippers should be. Instead, I see an ugly old pair of tatty dancing slippers – they're not even silver and do not match my outfit. I know I should be grateful that I have any slippers at all.

Mama is always telling me that I should be grateful for what I have in life, not what I haven't. But then again, she's not dancing in a proper dance competition. Great-Aunt Matooba says in the UK children have too much and are ungrateful, and if my great-aunt says it, then it must be so. But I do not believe her. I mean, how can she know what every child in the UK thinks? I'm sure there are many who are grateful for what they have. If you are grateful, please write and let me know. Don't expect a quick reply; our postal service is a bit slow, and the UK is a long, long way away.

The audience's applause for the last group has died down. Now it is our turn. My heart leaps into my mouth again. Not literally, of course; that would be most strange, horrible, and quite scary too, I think. Literally. Do you know this word? It is another word we have just learned in Advanced English, English. It means it happens for real. But I expect you know this already.

"Ladies and gentlemen, the next group to perform are the Mall Hall Stompers. Please give a warm welcome to" . . .

We're on, wish me luck; I'm going to need it.

Chapter 24

The performance

 Strange as it may seem, things are going well. I am dancing and keeping up with the others. Our dance routine, one of two, is being well received, judging by the applause which means clapping, as you may or may not know.

Perhaps Uncle is right; I don't need the magic slippers after all. I can see Great-Aunt Matooba and Mama in the audience. Their smiling faces tell me all I need to know. Twani and the people of the village have great big grins on their faces. My heart swells with pride, and my face beams like moonbeams – you know this expression?

Then it happens. In our second dance, our impression of modern dance is to the tune of Hakuna Matata, which means in Swahili 'no worries.'

Everything falls apart.

Like a crazy elephant, my feet no longer obey me. As the group goes one way, I go the other. I crash into the girl next to me. She swears in Swahili. I turn the other way and collide with the boy on the other side, sending him spinning like a top. Yes, we do have boys, but few, sadly.

Now the audience is laughing. They are looking directly at me. My cheeks are red with shame. Before I knew what was happening, I had run off and did not stop until I reached home, which is quite a long way, I can tell you. Ignoring the stares from passers-by at the girl with the sparkling tutu, with tears streaming down her cheeks, I reach home. My replacement dancing slippers were ruined, of course.

Chapter 25

Moonlight

When I get home, my costume filthy and dirty, I go straight to my room which I share with my sister and lay down on my bed, crying my head off.

Later, my Mama, Great-Aunt Matooba, and even my brothers and sister try to console me, but it's no use. I have ruined my chances of ever winning the K.N.D.C. Our dance club will be . . . dis . . .qual . . . Oh, you look it up. In my mind, I see the skanky girls crowing over my failure. If only I had had the silver slippers, then none of this would have happened.

Mama tries to sooth my feelings with some homemade soup, but I cannot eat and remain in my room until I'm all cried out and I fall into a fitful sleep. Tomorrow is day two of the competition, but it is no use. It will happen again, or so I think.

I wake with a start. I do not know how long I have been asleep, but the room is bathed in a bright light. It is too early for morning. I get up, trying not to wake my sleeping sister. I stare out of the open, glassless window. Oh, my gosh . . . It is the moon. It is gigantic. I have never seen it so bright before.

Before me is the biggest moon I think I have ever seen, and when you think we have pretty big moons here in Africa, I'm talking about gigantic. I don't mean that the moon here is bigger than your moon, because it's the same moon. It's just that here in Africa, we are near the equator, which means we are closer to the moon than you are; hence, it seems bigger. One day, I hope you will all be able to come to Kenya and see the moon from here. Until then, you will have to take my word for it.

I'm looking at the moon. And the moon is looking at me, or rather, the face of the moon is looking back at me. Face? Yes, there is definitely a face with eyes, a nose, and a mouth, and it is speaking.

What the . . .?

I can hear what it says.

"You don't need magical slippers, child: you just need to believe in yourself."

And the moon winks.

Did the moon wink?

I think it did. The moon is replaced with the face of the lion, and the lion is nodding. I stare at the images for what it seems like forever, then I go back into bed and try to fall asleep.

This is just a dream within a dream, which I repeat over and over to myself. It certainly works better than counting sheep. Great-Aunt Matooba says there are more sheep in the UK than people. So, if they cannot sleep, they count sheep.

I imagine people who cannot sleep going out in the middle of the night to find a field with sheep in it. No, this cannot be right; I don't think this is what Great-Aunt Matooba means. I think she is using a meta . . . meta, that's it, a met/a/phor.

"Yolonde, wake up."

Mama is knocking on the door to our room. My sister rubs her eyes while my brothers sleep soundly.

"What is it, Mama?"

"Get dressed quickly; Uncle is here, and he has some news for you. Quickly, child, quickly."

Chapter 26

The slippers return

I get dressed hastily. Uncle is standing in the doorway, his cap in his hand. His face is beaming. I sense good news, but I'm not sure what it could be.

"Yolonde, child, I have great news. We have found your magic slippers." Uncle produces the slippers from behind his back.

"What? Where did you find them?" I am overcome with emotion and joy. I run over and give Uncle the biggest hug.

"OK," he says, laughing.

"Where did you find them?"

He suddenly becomes serious. "In the locker of Sumba."

I cannot believe it. Why would she do that? Of course, I can well believe it; it's just the sort of thing the skank girls would do.

"She will be punished for this, Yolonde; don't worry about that. The most important thing is that you can re-enter the competition."

"But how, Uncle? I ran off, and we've surely been dis . . . disqualified?" Got it!

Uncle chuckles: you know this word? It means to have a little laugh. In the UK, Great-Aunt Matooba says there is a comedy act called the Chuckle Brothers, so I guess you must have heard of it.

"Well, in spite of your somewhat unorthodox dance routine, we actually came third in the group category. And there's still the individual and pairs to dance for."

I look at my uncle. "Unortho . . . what? It doesn't matter; we still cannot win now."

"No, Yolonde, that's where you are quite wrong," says Uncle. "The first three winners go through to the K.N.D.C., so there's everything to dance for."

Huh! Am I hearing what I'm thinking I'm hearing? I stare for a long time at my uncle, and then my senses return. "Well, don't just stand there, Uncle; we have a competition to win. I lock arms with Uncle, and we head out to his OMG, he has a gari – a car. I wink at my astonished family as I walk past.

"Come on, there's room for you all, but we must hurry."

Chapter 27

The final

 I'm back in the game. Not only back but winning. My partner Nguro and I nail the pairs with a nifty bolero and finish off with a smart paso doble. Then it's the individuals. I thought long and hard about what my entry should be, finally settling on a medley of classic and modern dance with a twist.

I have a sequence where I am pretending to dance with the lion, although of course the lion is not there. I show it to my sister and brothers, and they think it is hil . . . very funny. Let's hope the audience and judges feel the same. At this stage, both the judges and the audience have a vote.

Well, all is going brilliantly, and then I come to the lion sequence, and I hear the laughter. I'm not sure whether the audience is laughing at me or finding it genuinely funny and laughing with me.

After the previous disasters, I have learned not to allow myself to be put off by the audience's reaction, even if it is favourable, for then, as Uncle says, you must avoid becoming too confident because then you make mistakes anyway. With a last flourish, I finish and wait. I am greeted by silence.

Is this a good or bad thing?

The silence is unbearable. Then a clap, followed by another clap, then a deluge of claps. Deluge means downpour, by the way, like rain. A roar comes from the audience, and it is not from the lion. I gaze in amazlement – sorry, I was too excited to spell it properly, even if I could. There are people standing on their feet, cheering, applauding. My cheeks are red with pride.

Uncle, followed by Aunt Matooba and Mama, have come onto the stage and are throwing their arms around me. I cannot believe this is happening, but it is. Eventually the hubbub dies down, and we are joined on stage by the other dance groups. There is a hush as the winners and the runners-up are announced. The main judge, a most distinguished-looking gentleman with white hair and a beard, speaks.

"Ladies and Gentlemen." – This is the 1980s, after all.

"The winner of this year's group performance goes to the Watuzis." We clap our hands politely. It is important to be a good sport, hide our disappointment, and not become bitter. So, my Great-Aunt Matooba says.

Then the second and third places are announced, and of course we are not there. But we knew this anyway. Next is the turn of the pairs. First place goes to the Back Street Dance Troupe. My heart sinks and then soars as the judge announces second place. "Goes to the Mall Hall Stompers."

OMG! OMG! We have come second; I don't believe it. It means we are still in with a chance if, and it's a big if, we can win the individual category. Second place will not be enough. It must be first.

"It is my great pleasure to announce that the winner of the individual entry is Pasi of the Lothangi Dancing Club." Loud cheers from the audience and groans from myself and my fellow dancers. That's it then. All over. I look over and see the disappointment in Uncle's eyes and Mama's. Not to mention Great-Aunt Matooba, who looks as if something from a bird's bottom has just dropped onto her face. The din in the ballroom is deafening.

"Hello!"

Bang! Bang! Bang!

The chief judge is banging on his desk, his mic squeals. He is appealing for calm and quiet. After a time, the noise dies down, and we listen. "I'm most terribly sorry," he says, looking as if he wants the ground or at least a warthog to open its mouth and swallow him whole. "I'm afraid I've announced the results in the wrong order."

"Wot?"

"The actual . . . er, the actual winner is Yolonde of the Mall Hall Stompers."

OMG! OMG! OMG!

I can't believe it; I'm leaping up and down, hugging Mama, hugging Uncle, and hugging Great-Aunt Matooba. Maybe not hugging Great-Aunt Matooba, but she doesn't seem to mind. An appeal is lodged by the former winners, whose looks, if they were daggers, would obviously slaughter us all. After an agonizing wait of what seems like hours but is probably just a few minutes, it is confirmed.

We've won! We've won! We've won!

Chapter 28

Calm before the storm

Well, what can I tell you? After the excitement and celebrations – yes, I've learned that word – life returns to some sort of normal while we wait for the K.N.D.C., which is to be held in three months' time. I don't know what is normal for you, but for me, it means fetching the water, cleaning the house, feeding the chickens, annoying my brothers and sister with my practising, and attending school. Phew, it's a lot, I know.

Great-Aunt Matooba says children in the UK are also busy with their lives, but in a different way. Homework is their number one bugbear. Which reminds me I better go and do mine now otherwise I'll be in deep doo doo. You know this saying, I think. See you later . . .

Well, I'm back, and I've got so much to tell you since we last spoke that I don't know where to begin. Perhaps I should start where I left off. Firstly, and you are not going to believe this, but we came third. That is, our club, the Stompers, came third in the K.N.D.C., and wait for it, I came second in the individuals. Which means I have won a place at the prestigious New York Dance Academy, in the United States of America, or the USA, as you might know it. I know, it's absolutely amazing, isn't it?

Every day for the past week, I've been screaming at the top of my voice with excitement. Thank you, Lion; thank you, Magic Slippers; thank you, Moon. Thank you, Uncle, and the Dance Club. Thank you, Shop Aunty. But most of all, thank you to Mama and Great-Aunt Matooba for all the help and support. So, you see, I'm on top of the world, or so I should be, but for one thing. Money and my stepdad. Thank you for pointing out that, actually, it's two things. Which is why, after a week of tremendous joy, my face looks as if I've just fallen into a splat of elephant dung.

Chapter 29

Henri returns

The problem is this: Although I've won a place at the New York School of Dance and the Kenyan Government has genu . . . genu . . . awarded me a grant to study there, it only pays for part of the tuition and not accommodation – this one I had to look up in my dictionary. (Hey, I've just thought of a great way of remembering this one: two crocodiles and two monkeys.)

I expect you use dictionaries as well, although Great-Aunt Matooba says that in the UK, all children have access to a dictionary, but few make use of it. Is this true? I don't know, but if my aunt says it is, it must be so. "Not hungry enough," says my aunt. Whereas, here, we are always hungry for knowledge and often hungry for food too. (There are not always bananas on the trees, you know, and too much of a good thing can also make you sick.)

You see, we are always told that if you study hard, you can better yourself. Whatever that means, I think I understand. The same is true in the UK, I think, study hard and you will succeed. It is the same the world over, yes. Then why are so many out of work? I'm looking out of the window at the men sitting around with nothing to do. It's not all their fault if there isn't any work, but Mama says there's plenty of work in Nairobi. She says they are just lazy. But I think, why work if you don't have to?

Unemployment in the early 1980s in Kenya is extremely high. Great-Aunt Matooba says it is high in the UK too. There's something called a world recess . . . and a lot of people are out of work. You will have to write and let me know.

But what happens if we all become educated with degrees and other things? We can't all be brain surgeons, can we? I mean, someone has to sweep the streets and collect the rubbish. I couldn't believe it when my great-aunt told me that in the UK, every household has their rubbish collected from their house. That is amazing, if true. Then again, everything my aunt says is true, isn't it?

In Nairobi, they do have rubbish bin collectors, but out here in the sticks, we have to take our rubbish to the dump, which is on the edge of the village. (OMG, when the wind blows in the wrong direction!)

How does my aunt know these things? She is truly an amazing woman. I'm thinking these things while staring out of the glassless window, waiting for Henri, my stepdad, who, Mama says, is coming to see us and hopefully take me, my sister, and my brothers out.

So, here I am sitting in my Sunday best, and everyone is excited. Mama is cooking a special meal of Wali, and all the aunts and Great-Aunt Matooba are here helping Mama in the kitchen. Yes, I know, even Aunt Matooba.

The reason. Mama has invited Henri to dinner, which is a good way to lure Henri here as he loves a slap-up meal, especially when it's free. And of course, it is a special occasion, as Mama is going to tell Henri about my winning the competition and my place in the New York Dance Academy.

That is one reason.

The other reason is that we need Henri's permission for me to go. Under Kenyan law, as Henri is legally married to my mother, he has to agree, otherwise . . . Oh, that is the honk of the bus announcing its arrival. I watch as it grinds slowly to a halt in a spray of dust and exhaust fumes. The brakes squeal as if in pain, which, as it is so old, it probably is.

I continue to watch as the bus spews out its cargo of Saturday afternoon shoppers – lucky them – village kids, and a few men returning from Nairobi and the betting shops. I wait. Still, there is no sign of Henri. Please don't tell me he hasn't come. The last passengers have gotten off. I hear grumblings and shouts from within the bus, and at last there is Henri, lurching down the steps and swaying from side to side, clutching a half-empty bottle of whisky.

Oh, No!

Chapter 30

Henri says no

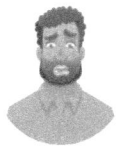 Yes, he is drunk.

So drunk he can barely stand up. I'm not surprised that he is struggling to remain on his feet given that Mama and Aunty are giving him such a hard time. It's called a tongue lashing. Here in Kenya, we ladies are particularly good at it, as I'm sure they are in the UK too.

"Drunken fool!" says my aunt.

Henri just growls.

Somehow, they manage to calm Henri down and get him seated at the table. Mama starts to bring out the food while Henri breaks off huge chunks of freshly baked bread and stuffs them into his open mouth. Yuck! I understand now why Mama is always telling me to eat with my mouth closed.

One only has to look at Henri throwing crumbs all over the table to see the sense in these words. Still, the bread seems to cheer him up somewhat, along with the second glass of whisky he is drinking.

Great-Aunt Matooba says it is the hairy dog. She sees my look of bafflement and explains that the hairy dog means that to cure a hangover from drinking too much, one should have another drink.

The logic escapes me, but if my Great-Aunt Matooba says it, then it must be so. Anyway, after he has whoofed down a second helping of Wali, Henri seems quite amenable, so, I'm hopeful of a good outcome when Mama asks him the question. Amenable means willing to do what is asked. It is another long word I have just learned in Advanced English, English.

You may have noticed that I am using the word 'one' instead of 'you' when addressing somebody. This is something else I have just learned in Advanced English, English. The correct form of addressing a person in the present tense is apparently one.

I asked Great-Aunt Matooba about this, and she said that in the UK, everybody uses the term. I find this hard to believe.

"How is one today?

"Would one like a cup of tea?

"One has just dropped a smelly one."

It sounds silly to me. I think I'll stick with you; it's less posh.

Please write and let me know if it is true. Seriously, I just have, and judging by the filthy look Great-Aunt Matooba has just given me I'm in trouble. I think one needs to go to the loo. Aunty comes to my rescue.

"You are disgusting, Henri."

"What!" cries Henri, all innocent, which of course he is. I swiftly make my exit. When I return, all sweet and innocent, I notice a distinct change of atmosphere at the table.

Mama and Aunty took the opportunity of my absence to explain to Henri about the dance competition and allowing me to study in New York. My heart sinks. I have seen that look on Henri's face many times and know what it means.

Oh, poo!

Chapter 31

When the rock hits the bottom, the only way is up

 My eyes are red, my nose is snotty, and my face is wet from the endless tears as I realize that my dream is disappearing in front of me. Fortunately, we do not have mirrors in the house; otherwise, I would see how ugly I have become. You, of course, can see me. So, I apologize for my horrible look.

I feel as if my life has ended. No matter how much my brothers and sister try to comfort me, nothing will ever be the same again. I wish the ground would open up and swallow me whole. No, I wish it would open up and swallow Henri whole. I then realize that this will not help, as Henri, underground, will never be able to give his consent.

I appeal to Mama and Aunty. I scream at Henri, who just staggers around, looking sheepish. You know this saying; I mentioned it earlier. Mama takes me into the bedroom to calm me down.

"Come, Henri," says Aunty, "you and I need to take a walk." Henri starts to protest, but my aunt accepts no excuses and bundles him out of the hut. You see, Henri may be violent and a little truculent when drunk – I'll let you look this word up – I'm too upset to explain it now. Anyway, as I said, Henri can be quite nasty, but he is still only a slightly built man with skinny shoulders, whereas my aunt . . .

I think you get the idea, as my aunt has literally thrown him through the open door. Henri staggers out, squinting into the sunshine. My aunt follows, slamming the door behind her. Their voices become quieter as it becomes clear that they are walking away from the hut. Where they are going, I do not know and do not really care. I rush to my room, slamming the door, and I don't let my brothers or sister in. Mama tells them to leave me alone. I sob violently and stop only when I have cried myself to sleep.

The next thing I know, I'm sitting under the Joob, Joob, tree again. It is daylight and the air is fresh and crisp, which means early morning. Although I expect that in the UK you would consider it quite warm. Is it possible to sense air and freshness in dreams? I don't know, but this is a dream, isn't it?

A voice distracts me.

"Why so sad?"

I look up, and there is my friend the lion sitting on the lowest and thickest branch of the tree. That's a good thing because the lion is huge. I don't know how the tree is supporting his weight. But then again, in dreams, crazy things happen. Lion listens while I retell my tale of woe and despair. When I finish, the lion looks at me thoughtfully.

"That is a very sad tale, you know what you should always do when you feel sad?"

"No, says I," thinking, is this really happening or is this a dream? Because it seems and feels real.

"Dance, of course," says the lion, as he jumps down in front of me, goes up onto his hind legs, and extends a paw.

I rise to my feet and accept.

Lion takes me through his dance routine using many of the steps and dances, which, of course, thanks to Lion I now know.

Eventually, exhausted and out of breath, we paused. Yes, I did say paused, not paws.

"How do you feel now?" asks the lion while I sit back down under the tree, and the lion leaps back onto the branch to shield himself from the sun.

"I feel much better now, thank you, Lion." And I do. It's amazing. All my cares and worries have suddenly vanished.

"You see, Yolonde."

He knows my name.

"The way to tackle things when you are down is to go to your special place, and then you see things more clearly."

Wow, the lion is being very deep today, almost like a philoso-lion.

"What do you mean?"

"Well, Yolonde, it's not what happens to you that's important. It's how you react to it."

"I'm sorry." I think this lion is talking in riddles.

"You always have a choice: to accept what has happened to you or to do something about it."

"And what can I do?" This is getting annoying now.

"Firstly, you can choose not to react."

"How does that help exactly?"

"Or . . . you can do something about it," says the lion scratching a flea.

"Like what!" Yes, I know I'm raising my voice a little here.

"Stay positive, keep calm, and carry on. Something will turn up; it always does. It's all about how you look at life," says the lion, his voice fading.

Before I can remon . . . remon . . . argue back, the lion vanishes, as does the tree. My eyes open. It's dark and I'm back in my room.

What has just happened.'

Chapter 32

New York, New York, so good they named it twice

Well, it's three months later, and here I am in New York, New York. Did you know it's so famous that they named it twice? My head is giddy and reeling; the buildings are colos . . . colos . . . Really big. No mud huts here, Aunty. They have skyscrapers, which look down on other skyscrapers. And my head hurts as I try to look up and see the tops of some of them. It's almost impossible.

I'm staying with a local family that is connected with the School of Dance. They're really nice and have helped me settle in, but how can I describe this to you, the noise, the traffic, the hustle, the bustle? It makes Nairobi seem like a backwater. Not really, Nairobi is also very hustle-and-bustle. But New York is different, and, as for the people, they are so big. Except for the Maasai, of course. I have never seen such people; they even make Kenyan grandmothers seem tiny. And do you know what the funny thing is? After a while, you get used to it, and it seems almost normal.

I bet you're wondering how I got here. In the end, in return for a year's supply of whisky, Henri agreed to let me go. He didn't really have much choice, as my aunt threatened him with all kinds of horrible happenings if he refused. When it comes to it, whisky usually does it with Henri.

So, here I am, goggled-eyed and breathless, about to start my first lesson. It really is a dream come true, and thanks to my aunt and the village having a whip round and the grant from the Kenyan Government, I don't have to worry about fees and such, so long as I pass my studies, of course.

One can live quite cheaply in New

York, so long as one doesn't spend any money. (There's that word *one* again.) I miss Mama, Aunty, my brothers and sister, and the village, of course. But I do write home regularly, so it's not so bad. Sometimes, to pursue your dreams, you have to make sacrifices.

"That's what life's all about," says Aunty.

Anyhoo, I bet you're dying to see my schedule, so I thought I'd show you. This is the timetable for my first year:

Dance Theory. History of dance. Basic Steps. The Classics: rhumba, tango, and ballroom. And of course, modern dance, jazz, street, and hip-hop, plus an introduction to ballet (balance and stretching).

Cool, eh? It's full-on. There is no time for anything else. To succeed, you have to make sacrifices, and as everyone has made sacrifices for me, I can hardly let them down now, can I? My favourite lessons are tap and ballet. Wow, it's really hard, particularly what they call point-to-point, which really hurts your toes, and hip-hop. Well, it has got to be trendy, eh?

This is Jane. She says hi. She's also at school studying dance and acting. We've become besties. She's been showing me New

York, well, when we have time, and introducing me to something called a bagel and hot dogs, which I have never heard of. I'm ashamed to admit this to Jane, but I don't mind you knowing. (When Jane first told me about hot dogs, I thought people in New York were barbarians.)

I mean, in Kenya, we would never dream of roasting a dog. Boy was I relieved and a little sheepish, I have to admit, when Jane bought me my first hot dog to try. I mean, nobody eats dogs, right? Right? You won't tell her now, will you? I enjoyed the bagel; the taste was amazing, but you can keep the hot dogs. I much prefer my Mama's Kenyan cooking.

Fortunately, I am allowed to use the kitchen to cook my own dishes, although I also have some meals with my host family. If I ate what New Yorkers eat every day, that would be the end of my dancing career, I think.

Anyway, I've got to go, as Jane is taking me to see a performance of Swan Lake at a theatre on Broadway, New York's most famous square for theatres and performances. No doubt you have heard of it, but Jane laughed when she saw the blank expression on my face. Well, what did she expect? I've never heard of Broadway until now. And now it's my dream to perform there one day. I know I will. Catch you later.

Chapter 33

Broadway

I told you I'd catch you later, but I didn't say how much later, did I? I graduated from the academy and managed to secure a job with a famous dance touring group, and our final night is in New York.

My car has just pulled up outside the famous Shubert theatre on Broadway. It's the afternoon's final rehearsal for the evening's performance, and guess what? I'm the star of the show. OK, not quite, but I do get my very own solo spot towards the end of the show. Not bad, eh, for a girl from the sticks. (The sticks are what Americans call the back and beyond; boondocks is another word they have for off the beaten track.) Funny language, eh?

I give my hi-fives to the other cast members as I head towards the dressing room. The other dancers are already there and limbering up.

Curtains are up in ten, so I have to be ready. Please excuse me while I get changed. It's a modern dance number, and the theme is Fagin. I'm the Artful Dodger, whatever that means. They did try to explain it, but I'm no wiser. (It's based on a story by a famous Vic . . . Vic . . . an old writer called Dickens.) I expect you to know more about it than I do, being that you are from the UK, the land of the Artful Dodgers. (That's just my little joke.)

I'm almost ready; I've just got to put my magic slippers on. I know what you're thinking: how can I wear dancing slippers if I'm supposed to look like someone from the 19th century? Have you not followed this story? Did I not say they were magic slippers?

I know; I was astonished when it first happened. Whatever routine I was supposed to be doing, the slippers would change to fit the routine. I couldn't believe it either. If it were ballet, I would open up the box, and there would be a pair of ballet shoes staring back at me. Or, as now, black hob-nail boot dance shoes.

All I have to do is open the box, and there they are. Still magical, obviously. I hide the box, of course; people might get suspicious to see a different pair of dancing shoes for each number in the same box. That's what I'm doing now, rummaging at the bottom of my dance kit bag for the box. And guess what? It is not there. Well, the box is there, but not the slippers.

Chapter 34

A star is born

Stunned is not the word. I keep rummaging, hoping above all that they will turn up, but no. Then I remembered that I had taken the slippers out of the box the night before to give them a good clean. I can't blame the skank girls this time, can I?

Do you know what it's like to have a panic attack? I do. My chest does. My heart is pounding. I'm struggling to breathe; my tongue is drier than the driest riverbed in Kenya, and that's saying something. I must have fainted. How do I know this? People are gathering around me. Someone gave me a sip of water.

"Are you all right, Yolonday?" It's the American dance director, and he never says my name right. I explained my predicament. (It means what's happened.) That's how I see it, anyway.

Sighs of relief all around. "Is that all, Yolonday? We'd thought you'd had a heart attack," says the director.

Really?

Replacement dancing shoes are sent for in my size. My head is patted.

"Nothing to see here; all good now."

You think . . .

I sat dazed and alone. What am I going to do now? Without my magic slippers, I'm sunk. I slump back and close my eyes, trying to think.

"On in five!" shouts the stagehand.

"You don't need magic slippers, Yolonde. You just need to believe in yourself."

I open my eyes, and there is Lion. He is smiling at me. Lion fades and is replaced by the moon.

"You have the talent, Yolonde," says the moon. "You don't need magic slippers." The moon fades.

"You only have to believe, Yolonde." This time it's Great-Aunt Matooba. Mama is there too, and she's smiling.

"You're right," I said, as I jump up and shout, "Yay!"

"Are you OK?" says a startled fellow dancer as he stumbles backwards away from the mad girl.

It's time to go.

"I'm fine," says I, as I head out towards the stage and the curtain goes up.

The applause is deafening. The stage is strewn with flowers. The audience is up on their feet and shouting.

Shouting my name.

"Yolonde! Yolonde!"

I have just danced the dance of a lifetime. The whole performance by the dance troupe was simply magical. Well, I can't take all the credit now, can I?

I look down at my feet. I have borrowed a different pair of dancing shoes for every routine. And each time my performance is perfect. Sorry, our performance is perfect. So, I didn't need magic slippers after all. Just me.

The last standing ovation ends, and I skip back to the dressing room, floating as if on a cloud. The cloud gets better and better. As I open the door to the dressing area, I scream.

177

Aunty and Mama are both there with the biggest grins I have ever seen. I jump up and down with joy. How? "What are you doing here?" I finally managed to splutter. We hugged each other so tightly that I think we are all going to stop breathing.

"Your aunt paid for the tickets, Yolonde." Mama is beaming.

"Did you think we'd miss your greatest performance?" Both Mama and Aunty are laughing. Tears of joy stream down my cheeks.

Everyone is congratulating me on my performance.

"We need to talk about your contract, Yolonday, your permanent contract," says the art director. I look around, speechless. This is the greatest moment of my life. Can it ever be better than this? The answer comes when the door opens and the biggest bunch of flowers I've ever laid eyes on enters the room.

Oh! Yes, it can!

Chapter 35

Katrina,
as one-story ends, another begins

Grandma Wei, Wei, finally finishes telling her tale.

"That sounds unbelievable, Grandma."

"Well, you know what us Kenyans are like for telling tall stories, Katrina."

I shake my head. "But is it true?" I really, really would like to believe it was, at least I hoped it was.

"That's for you to decide, child." Grandma Wei, Wei, smiled and looked at me in a funny way.

"Now, I think it's time for you to go, Katrina. I'm feeling rather tired."

Three months later, Mum and I are going through Grandma Wei, Wei's, things, trying to decide which items to keep and which to chuck. Mum noticed the sad look on my face.

"She passed peacefully in the night. A good death, as they say in Kenya."

Here too, I think.

"Katrina, would you like to make a start on the bedroom? Begin by handing down those things on top of the wardrobe."

I take a stool and climb up to have a look. There are hatboxes, mostly empty, and a shoebox. I wondered why Grandma would keep a shoebox on top of the wardrobe and not below with the rest of her shoes. I take the box down and blow off the dust. There is a stencilled picture of a pair of silver slippers on the top of the lid. Intrigued, I slowly opened the box and peeked inside. And there they were. I was holding in my hands an incredibly old pair of dancing slippers – silver slippers.

"I will, Mum."

I looked at the slippers again. They were what they were – just an old pair of dancing slippers. But I knew they meant a lot to Grandma Wei, Wei. Don't get me wrong. I was trying to get my head around the fact that it was Grandma who was the girl with the magic dancing slippers.

Grandma Wei, Wei, is, was, Yolonde.

Grandma had won those competitions.

Grandma was the girl in the story, which she had been retelling over all these weeks. Wow!

I glanced again at the slippers, turning them over in my hands.

"Shame about the magic bit."

"What did you say?"

"Oh, nothing, Mum."

And then it happened. As I held them, the slippers began to glow and sparkle. Little stars twinkled all around the slippers, a glittery, silvery shower of sparks. I stared at the slippers not quite believing what my eyes were showing me.

"Mum."

"What is it, Katrina?"

"Did you know about these slippers, that Grandma was Yolonde and won lots of competitions?"

"Yes, child, your grandmother was world famous for a while."

"But her name's not Yolonde."

"Did you ever ask her what her first name was?"

"Er . . ."

I thought about this one; it's true, I'd only ever known Grandma as Grandma Wei, Wei.

"But why didn't you tell me? Why didn't Grandma tell me?"

"Because Grandma didn't want to talk about it, and we have to respect her wishes.

Besides, it was a long time ago."

Not that long ago surely, Grandma Wei, Wei, wasn't really that old not by Kenyan grandmother standards.

"So, why did she stop?"

"She had to choose."

"Choose, choose what?"

"Between her love for dancing and . . . well . . . love."

"I don't understand."

"She met and fell in love with your grandfather and wanted to have a family."

Something was still puzzling me.

"Couldn't she have done both?"

"Her life was very stressful; she had experienced fame and money and found that it wasn't quite what she thought it would be."

Being a kid, I, of course, focused on shallow things instead of the deeper meaning.

"She wasn't very old when she died, was she?" I was still looking at Grandma's picture; it was not the picture of an old lady. And Grandma Wei, Wei, never seemed old to me.

"No, Katrina, sixty-two is not considered old these days." I helped Mum put some stuff in a box.

"What did she die of?" Sometimes kids just don't know when to keep their mouths shut.

"Her heart was weak. She didn't know it, but what with all the dancing and the stress, it caught up with her, I guess."

I looked again at the picture of the young girl in the dancing costume.

"What did she do with all the money?"

See, I told you. Shallow.

I looked around at Tottenham's finest home for the elderly. Well, she was retired anyway; she wasn't elderly as such. There are many young grandmas these days. Grandma's flat was small and sparsely furnished. It wasn't exactly the Ritz.

Mum sighed; this was obviously a conversation she did not want to have. "She spent it creating wells and water courses – for her village and for the other villages of her tribe. It wasn't really a great deal of money and was soon gone."

I looked again at the bare flat, which had been my grandmother's home for so long. The cogs in my brain began to whirl.

"So, why live here? I mean, why not stay in Kenya?" My mum looked at me and shook her head.

"Yolonde met her future husband while she was on a dancing tour. There used to be an old ballroom and concert hall called the Palais de Dance. That's where your grandfather learned to dance. Tottenham is where your grandfather came from, and they decided to settle here."

"In Tottenham." I said, clearly astonished. I looked around at Grandma's Wei, Wei, possessions, it seemed so little to show for a lifetime. Mum seemed to read my thoughts.

"Bus drivers do not earn a fortune, child, even in London."

I couldn't think of anything else to say. My hands picked up the photo of Grandma Wei, Wei. The picture of Grandma's fairly slim and trim figure made me think of all those large Kenyan ladies. You never became a giant sponge pudding, did you, Grandma?

I looked once more at the magic slippers as they sparkled and shimmered in my hands. I turned the slippers over. Size five, my size.

"Mum, do you think I could have dancing lessons?"

The end.

Well, not quite...

The lion swished his tail. Well, it was still hot in the late afternoon sun, and the flies were beginning to bother him. The lioness was out hunting, and he found himself on his own.

Except for the cubs, who were busy playing games and mock fighting in the den.

Lion lay on his favourite rock near the Joob, Joob, tree. He stretched and rolled over. Life was good. It was cooler now, but only slightly. The lion looked about. But no creature stirred. Even the cubs were tired and were taking naps. Good. With a last swish of his tail, he got up and came down from the rock.

Lion stood in the little clearing and slowly raised himself onto two feet. Taking a last look around, he started tapping out a rhythm with his left foot and then began to dance.

"Ta ta, ta ta, ta ta, ta, ta ta da, ta; ta, da, ta, da, ta, da, dah, ah-hah. Boom!"

Now it's the end.

Here is a full list of the words which Yolonde found difficult to spell:

Page:

30	ditermened	determined
64	haluc	hallucinations
64	superst	superstition
76	suffo	suffocate
79	extrem	extremists
129	dis	disqualified
146	genu	genuinely
147	recess	recession
156	truculent	angry
169	Vic	Victorian
169	19thCen	century
	Silly bulls	syllables

If you would like to write to me then my address is:

Yolonde
Matobi village
Nairobi
Kenya

But as the mail is quite unreliable, you may also contact me via my English Fanclub:

Yolonde's Fan Club
C/O 13 Woodland Drive
Southwell
Notts. NG25 0DA

Or, my website
Yolonde
c/o https://www.michaelskyner.co.uk/

About The Author

Halloo

 If you have enjoyed this tale and would like to discover more about my books, then look me up on my website: michaelskyner.co.uk where you will discover many things, none of which are interesting or useful. But if you really are desperate to continue reading more of my work, then check out my books for **younger children:**

Chris Clotbo and the Conquest of the Americas.(silly)
The Spooky Tales of Blatherington Hall. (scary & silly)
The Monkey's Fart. (oh, for goodness' sake)

And for older readers:
Spirit Wolf. (dark and dystopian)
Space Nutz. (humorous sci fi or plain daft)

Available from:
Feedaread.com
Barnes and Noble.com

Amazon.co.uk
KPD Amazon.com (Kindle)
Local bookstore or from my website.

Bye-bye, for now.

About this story

I first discovered Kenya via an old schoolfriend called Kahn who introduced me to Kenya and its capital Nairobi. And who taught me so much about the harshness of life in the capital and also of the colourfulness and resilience of its people. Later I read a lot about Kenyan culture and life in the 1980's which is the setting for the book.

Yolonde is a children's fantasy story about hope and the human spirit, and hopefully some will find it funny.

I have tried to keep the book factually accurate but have taken some liberties to fit the story. The attack on the Westgate Mall for instance came much later in 2013, but I felt its inclusion was important to the story. If I have made any mistakes or misinterpretation, please forgive me.

And, although I write for children, I do not believe in sugar coating them from the world into which they are growing.